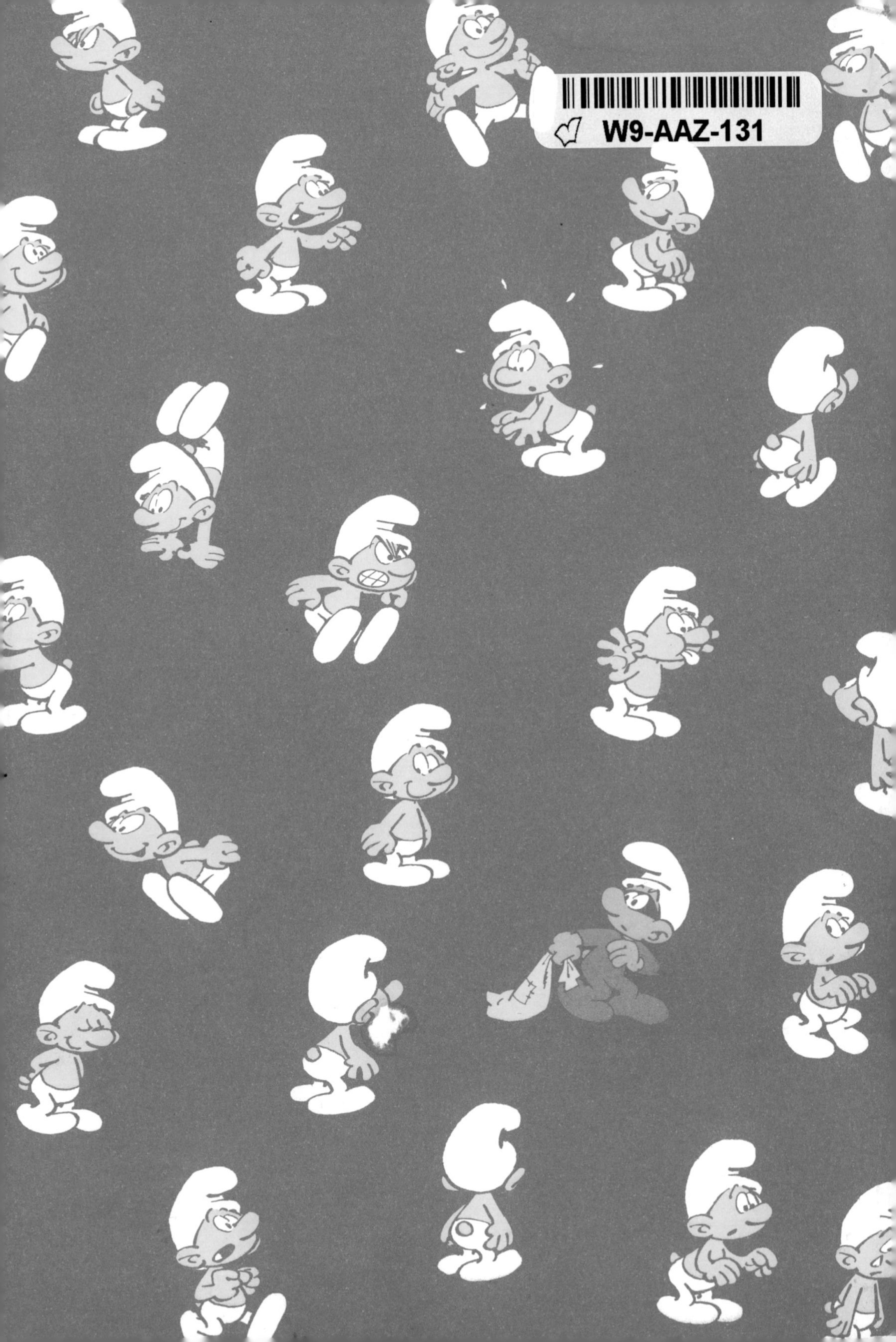

THE JEWEL SMURFER

Peyo

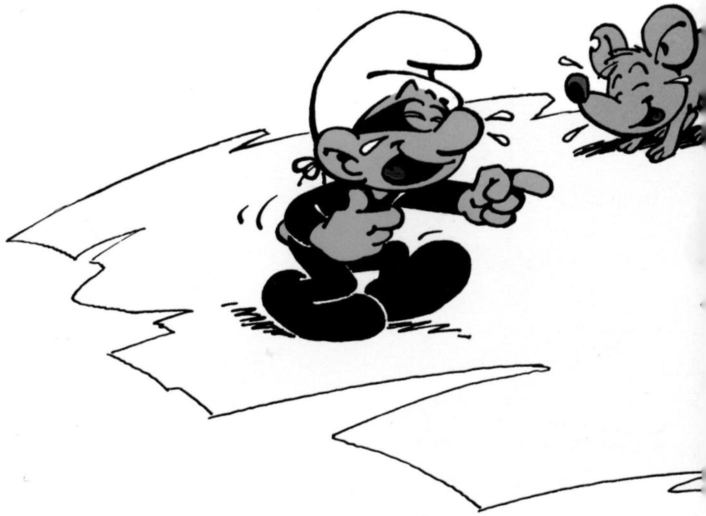

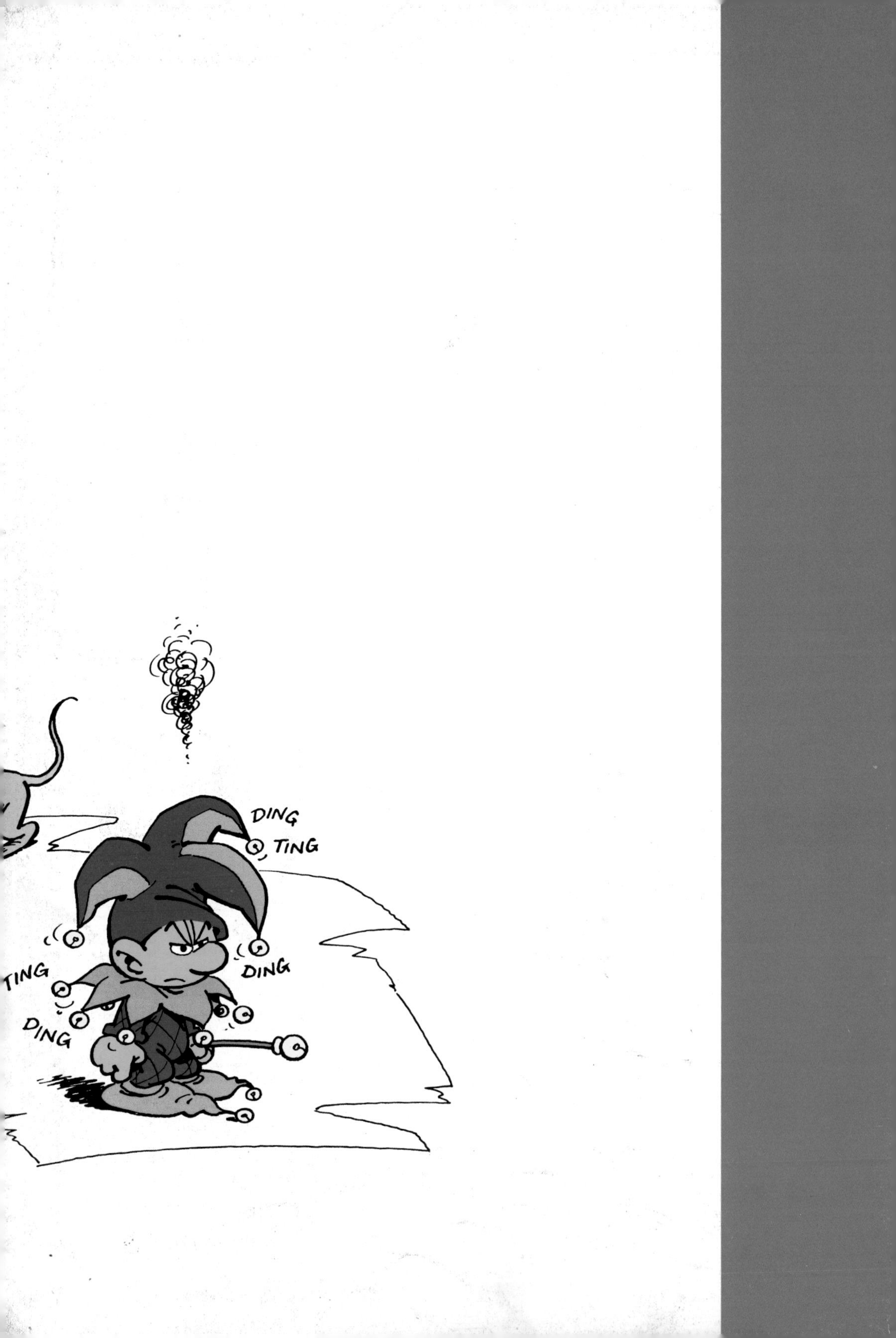
DING
TING
TING
DING
DING

THE JEWEL SMURFER

Okay, to the left or right?... For smurf's sake! Why don't humans smurf inside mushrooms like everybody else?

?

Let's see what's smurfing behind this door... ⸮Hmpf⸻!

Yum! The kitchen! Too bad Greedy Smurf isn't here!

?

⸮AAH!⸻

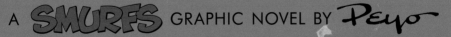

A **SMURFS** GRAPHIC NOVEL BY *Peyo*

WITH THE COLLABORATION OF
LUC PARTHOENS AND THIERRY CULLIFORD FOR THE SCRIPT,
ALAIN MAURY AND LUC PARTHOENS FOR ARTWORK,
NINE AND STUDIO LÉONARDO FOR COLORS.

PAPERCUTZ™

NEW YORK

 **SMURFS** GRAPHIC NOVELS AVAILABLE FROM **PAPERCUTZ** ™

1. **THE PURPLE SMURFS**
2. **THE SMURFS AND THE MAGIC FLUTE**
3. **THE SMURF KING**
4. **THE SMURFETTE**
5. **THE SMURFS AND THE EGG**
6. **THE SMURFS AND THE HOWLIBIRD**
7. **THE ASTROSMURF**
8. **THE SMURF APPRENTICE**
9. **GARGAMEL AND THE SMURFS**
10. **THE RETURN OF THE SMURFETTE**
11. **THE SMURF OLYMPICS**
12. **SMURF VS. SMURF**
13. **SMURF SOUP**
14. **THE BABY SMURF**
15. **THE SMURFLINGS**
16. **THE AEROSMURF**
17. **THE STRANGE AWAKENING OF LAZY SMURF**
18. **THE FINANCE SMURF**
19. **THE JEWEL SMURFER**

- **THE SMURF CHRISTMAS**
- **FOREVER SMURFETTE**

THE SMURFS graphic novels are available in paperback for $5.99 each and in hardcover for $10.99 each at booksellers everywhere. You can also order online at papercutz.com. Or call 1-800-886-1223, Monday through Friday, 9 – 5 EST. MC, Visa, and AmEx accepted. To order by mail, please add $4.00 for postage and handling for first book ordered, $1.00 for each additional book and make check payable to NBM Publishing. Send to: Papercutz, 160 Broadway, Suite 700, East Wing, New York, NY 10038.

THE SMURFS graphic novels are also available digitally wherever e-books are sold.

PAPERCUTZ.COM

THE JEWEL SMURFER
© Peyo - 2015 - Licensed through Lafig Belgium - www.smurf.com

English translation copyright © 2015 by Papercutz.
All rights reserved.

"The Jewel Smurfer"
BY PEYO
WITH THE COLLABORATION OF
LUC PARTHOENS AND THIERRY CULLIFORD FOR THE SCRIPT,
ALAIN MAURY AND LUC PARTHOENS FOR ARTWORK,
NINE AND STUDIO LÉONARDO FOR COLORS.

Joe Johnson, SMURFLATIONS
Adam Grano, SMURFIC DESIGN
Janice Chiang, LETTERING SMURFETTE
Matt. Murray, SMURF CONSULTANT
Jeff Whitman, SMURF COORDINATOR
Bethany Bryan, ASSOCIATE SMURFETTE
Jim Salicrup, SMURF-IN-CHIEF

PAPERBACK EDITION ISBN: 978-1-62991-194-6
HARDCOVER EDITION ISBN: 978-1-62991-195-3

PRINTED IN CHINA AUGUST 2015 BY WKT CO. LTD.
3/F PHASE 1 LEADER INDUSTRIAL CENTRE
188 TEXACO ROAD, TSEUN WAN, N.T., HONG KONG

Papercutz books may be purchased for business or promotional use. For information on bulk purchases please contact Macmillan Corporate and Premium Sales Department at (800) 221-7945 x5442.

DISTRIBUTED BY MACMILLAN
FIRST PAPERCUTZ PRINTING

THE JEWEL SMURFER

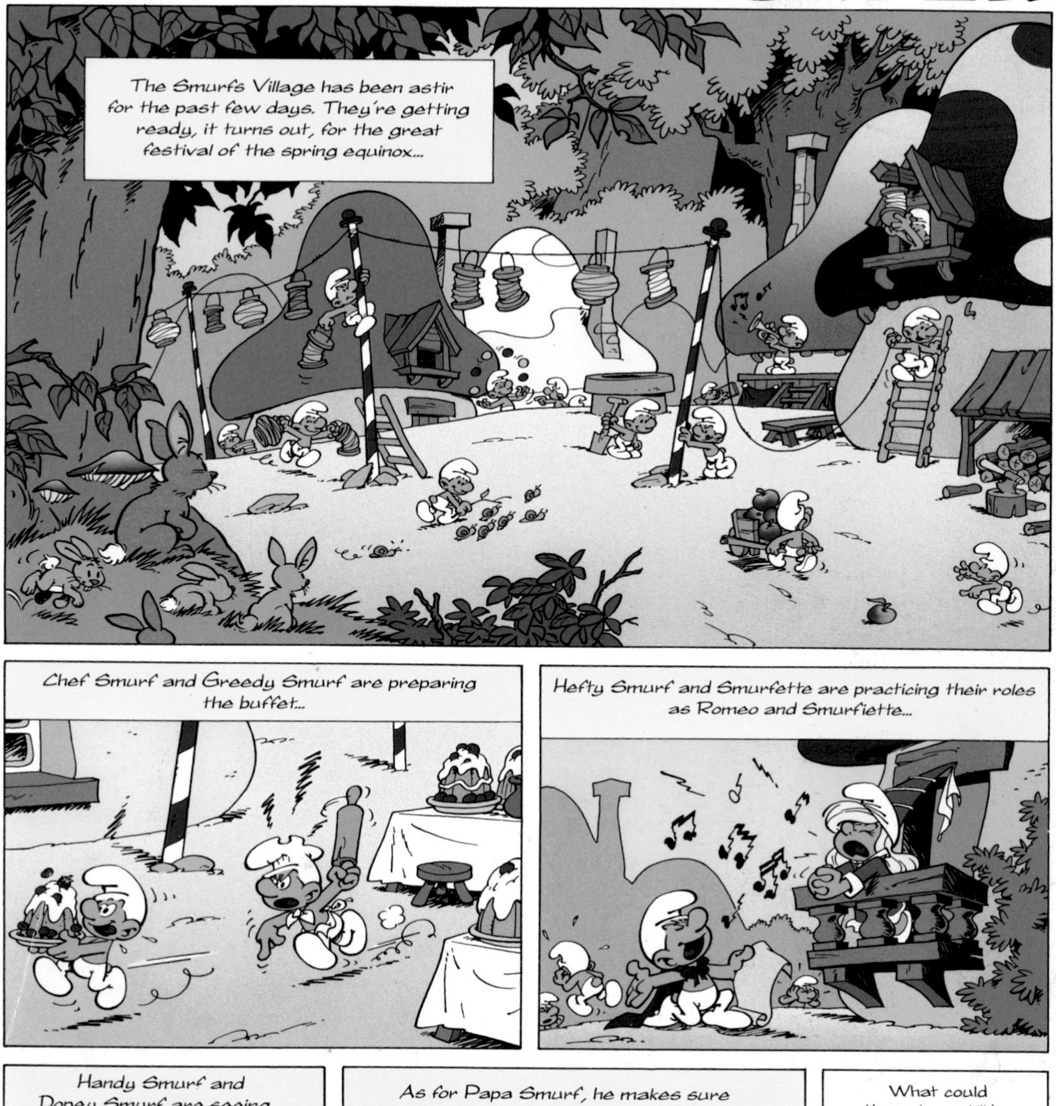

The Smurfs Village has been astir for the past few days. They're getting ready, it turns out, for the great festival of the spring equinox...
Chef Smurf and Greedy Smurf are preparing the buffet...
Hefty Smurf and Smurfette are practicing their roles as Romeo and Smurfiette...
Handy Smurf and Dopey Smurf are seeing to the decorations...
?
As for Papa Smurf, he makes sure everybody accomplishes his task...
Vanity Smurf, have you seen Brainy Smurf or Jokey Smurf?
Not since you smurfed them to the forest, Papa Smurf!
What could those two still be smurfing? I don't like them being that far from the village for so long!
© Peyo
1

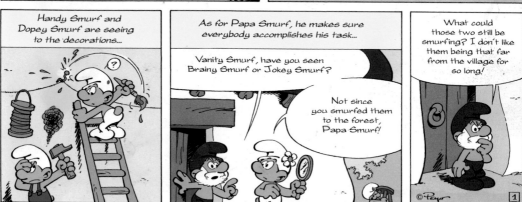

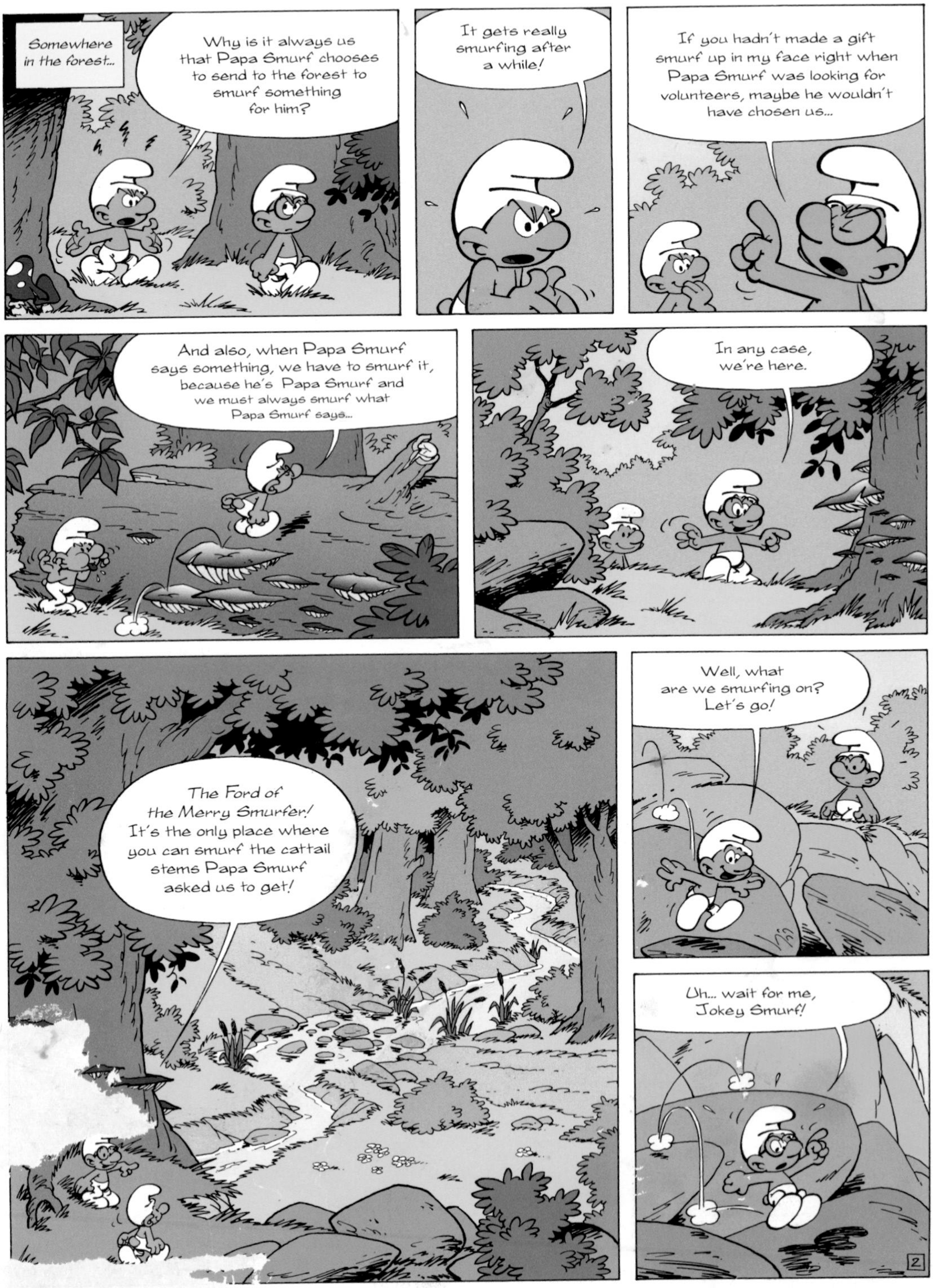
Somewhere in the forest...
Why is it always us that Papa Smurf chooses to send to the forest to smurf something for him?
It gets really smurfing after a while!
If you hadn't made a gift smurf up in my face right when Papa Smurf was looking for volunteers, maybe he wouldn't have chosen us...
And also, when Papa Smurf says something, we have to smurf it, because he's Papa Smurf and we must always smurf what Papa Smurf says...
In any case, we're here.
The Ford of the Merry Smurfer! It's the only place where you can smurf the cattail stems Papa Smurf asked us to get!
Well, what are we smurfing on? Let's go!
Uh... wait for me, Jokey Smurf!
2

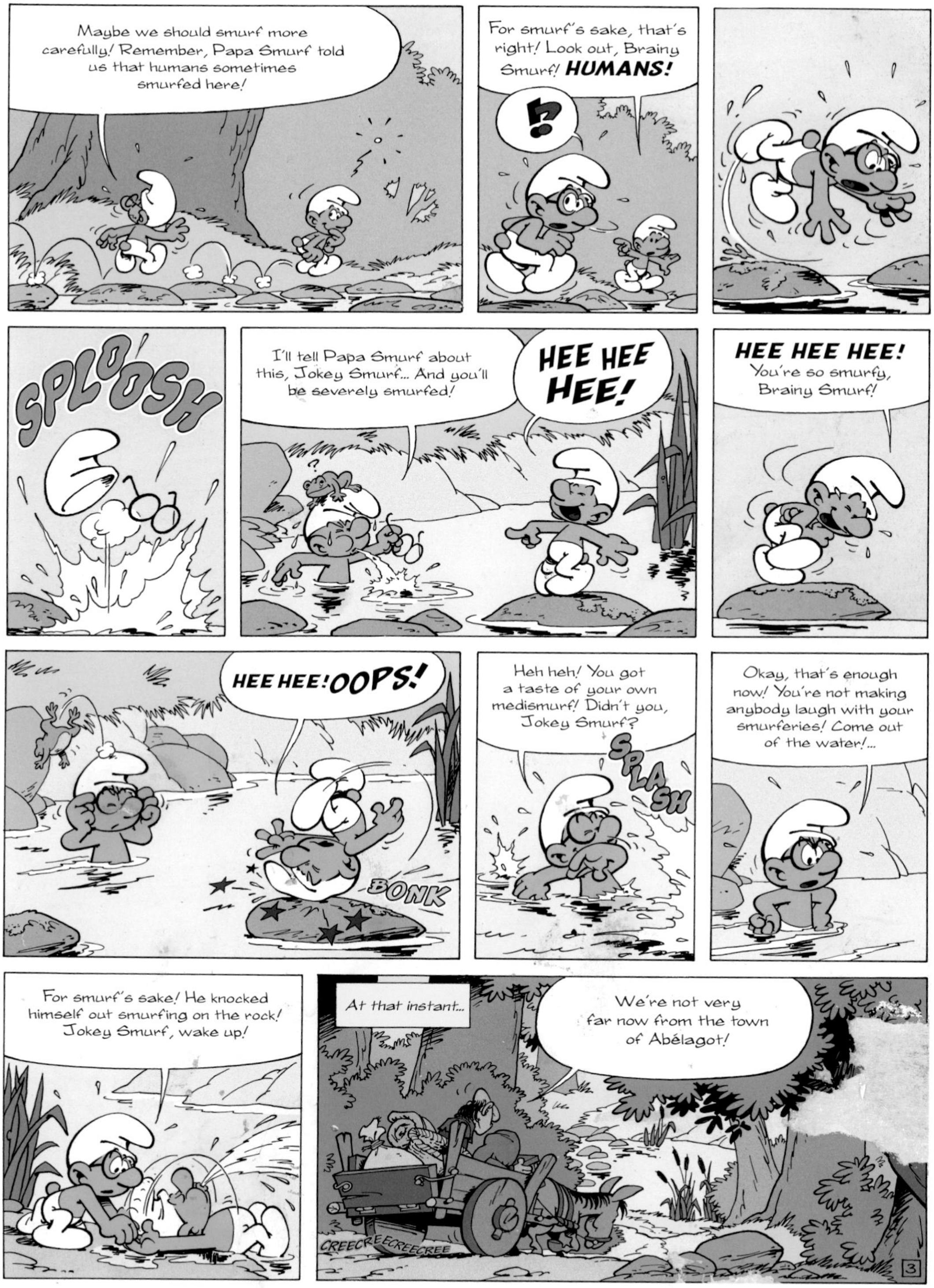

Maybe we should smurf more carefully! Remember, Papa Smurf told us that humans sometimes smurfed here!
For smurf's sake, that's right! Look out, Brainy Smurf! HUMANS!
!?
SPLOOSH
I'll tell Papa Smurf about this, Jokey Smurf... And you'll be severely smurfed!
?
HEE HEE HEE!
HEE HEE HEE! You're so smurfy, Brainy Smurf!
HEE HEE! OOPS!
BONK
Heh heh! You got a taste of your own medismurf! Didn't you, Jokey Smurf?
SPLASH
Okay, that's enough now! You're not making anybody laugh with your smurferies! Come out of the water!...
For smurf's sake! He knocked himself out smurfing on the rock! Jokey Smurf, wake up!
At that instant...
We're not very far now from the town of Abélagot!
CREECREECREECREE
3

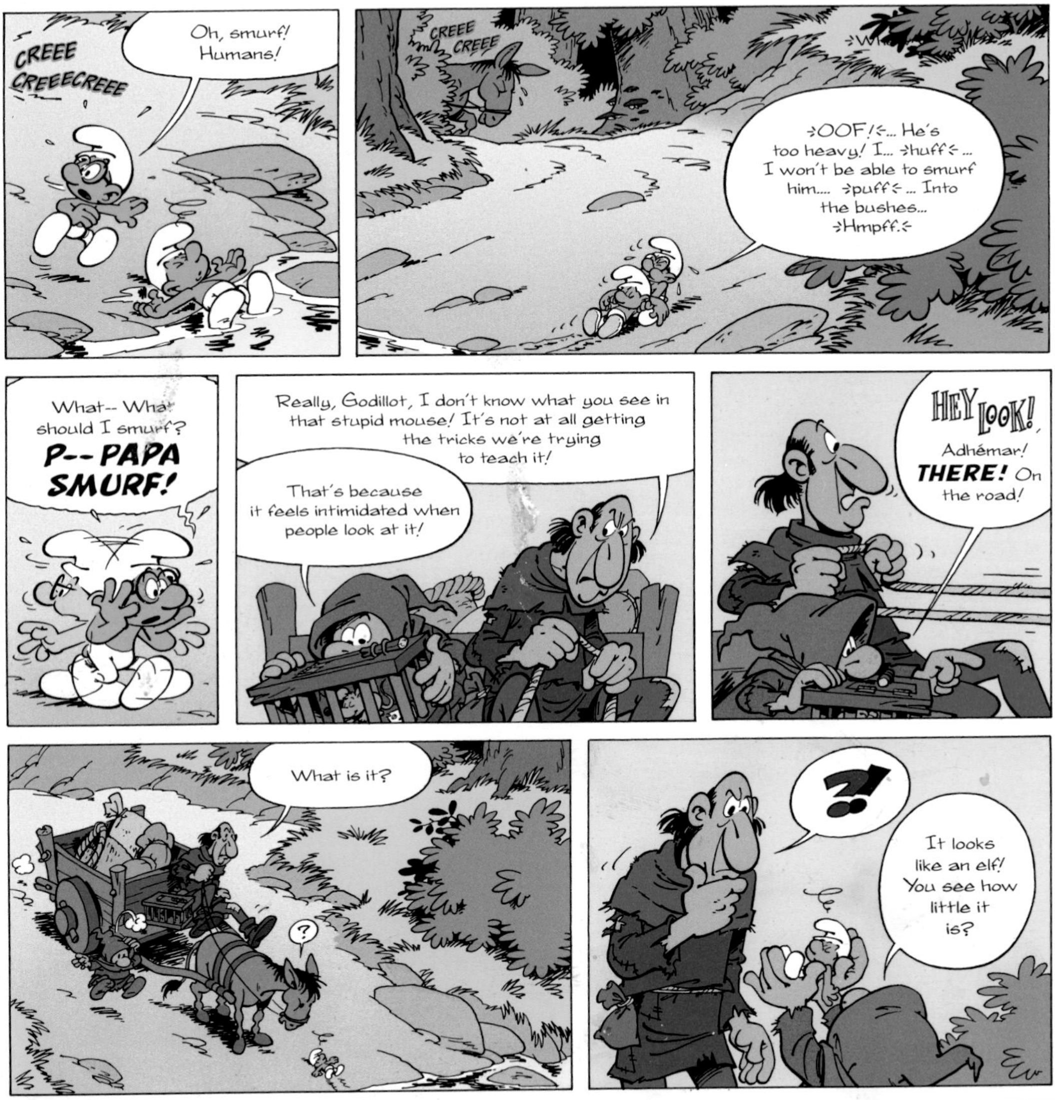
CREEE CREEECREEE
Oh, smurf! Humans!
CREEE CREEE
OOF!... He's too heavy! I... huff... I won't be able to smurf him.... puff... Into the bushes... Hmpff.
What-- What should I smurf? P--PAPA SMURF!
Really, Godillot, I don't know what you see in that stupid mouse! It's not at all getting the tricks we're trying to teach it!
That's because it feels intimidated when people look at it!
HEY LOOK! Adhémar! THERE! On the road!
What is it?
?
?!
It looks like an elf! You see how little it is?
Can I keep it, Adhémar?
Sure! But let's not linger here! If there's one elf, there may be others!... And I don't like that!
It's a catasmurfe! I absolutely must tell Papa Smurf!
© Peyo
4

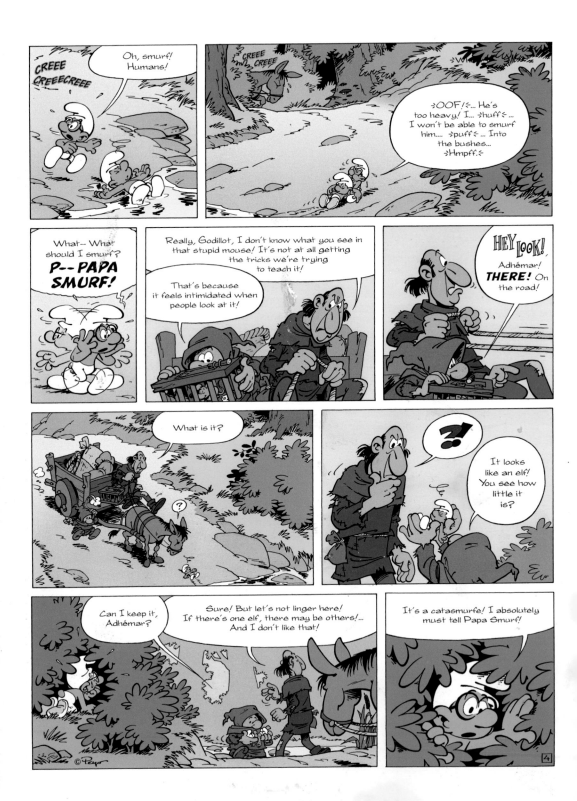

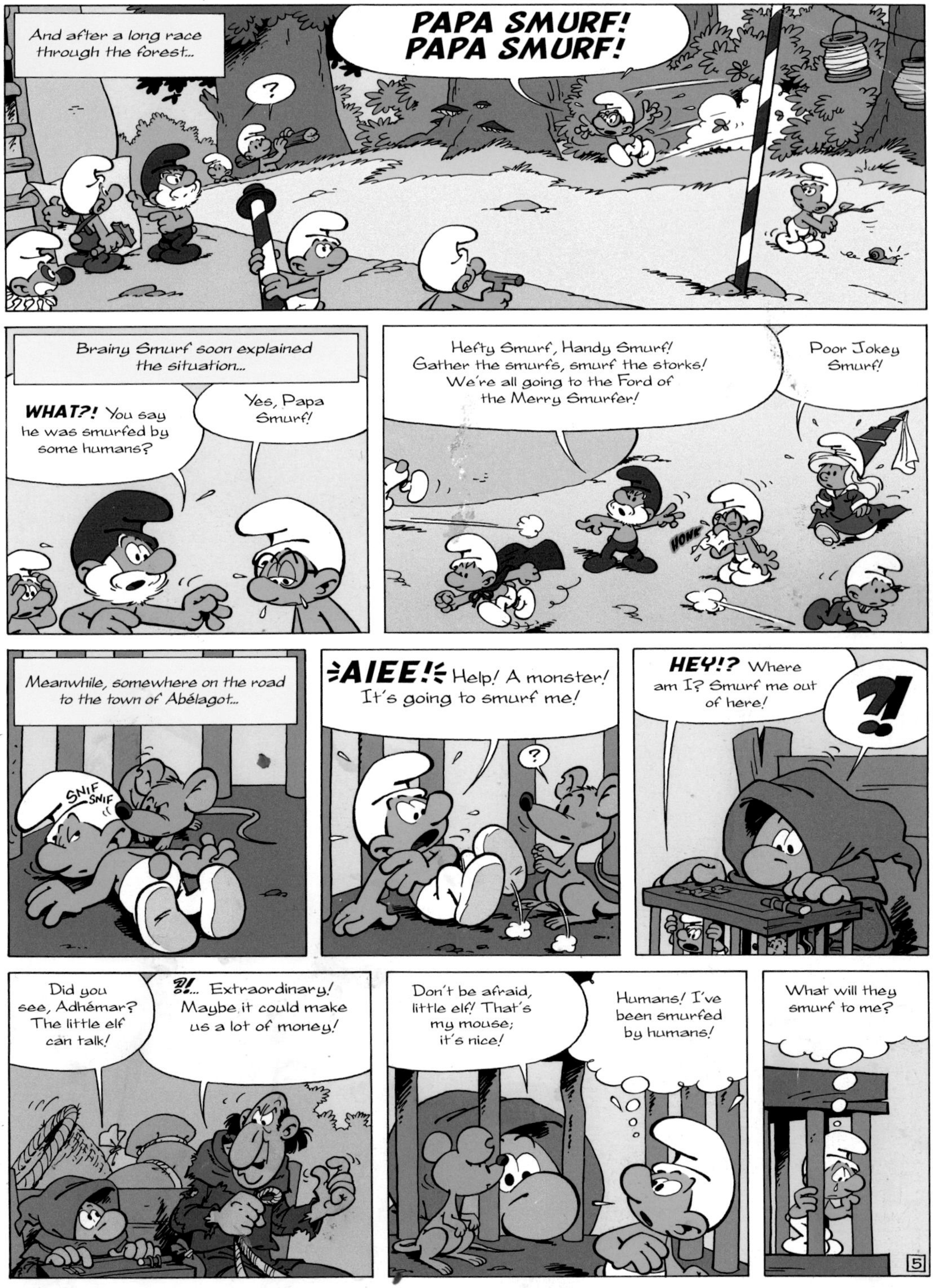
And after a long race through the forest...
PAPA SMURF! PAPA SMURF!
?
Brainy Smurf soon explained the situation...
WHAT?! You say he was smurfed by some humans?
Yes, Papa Smurf!
Hefty Smurf, Handy Smurf! Gather the smurfs, smurf the storks! We're all going to the Ford of the Merry Smurfer!
Poor Jokey Smurf!
HONK
Meanwhile, somewhere on the road to the town of Abélagot...
SNIF SNIF
AIEE! Help! A monster! It's going to smurf me!
?
HEY!? Where am I? Smurf me out of here!
?!
Did you see, Adhémar? The little elf can talk!
?!... Extraordinary! Maybe it could make us a lot of money!
Don't be afraid, little elf! That's my mouse; it's nice!
Humans! I've been smurfed by humans!
What will they smurf to me?
5

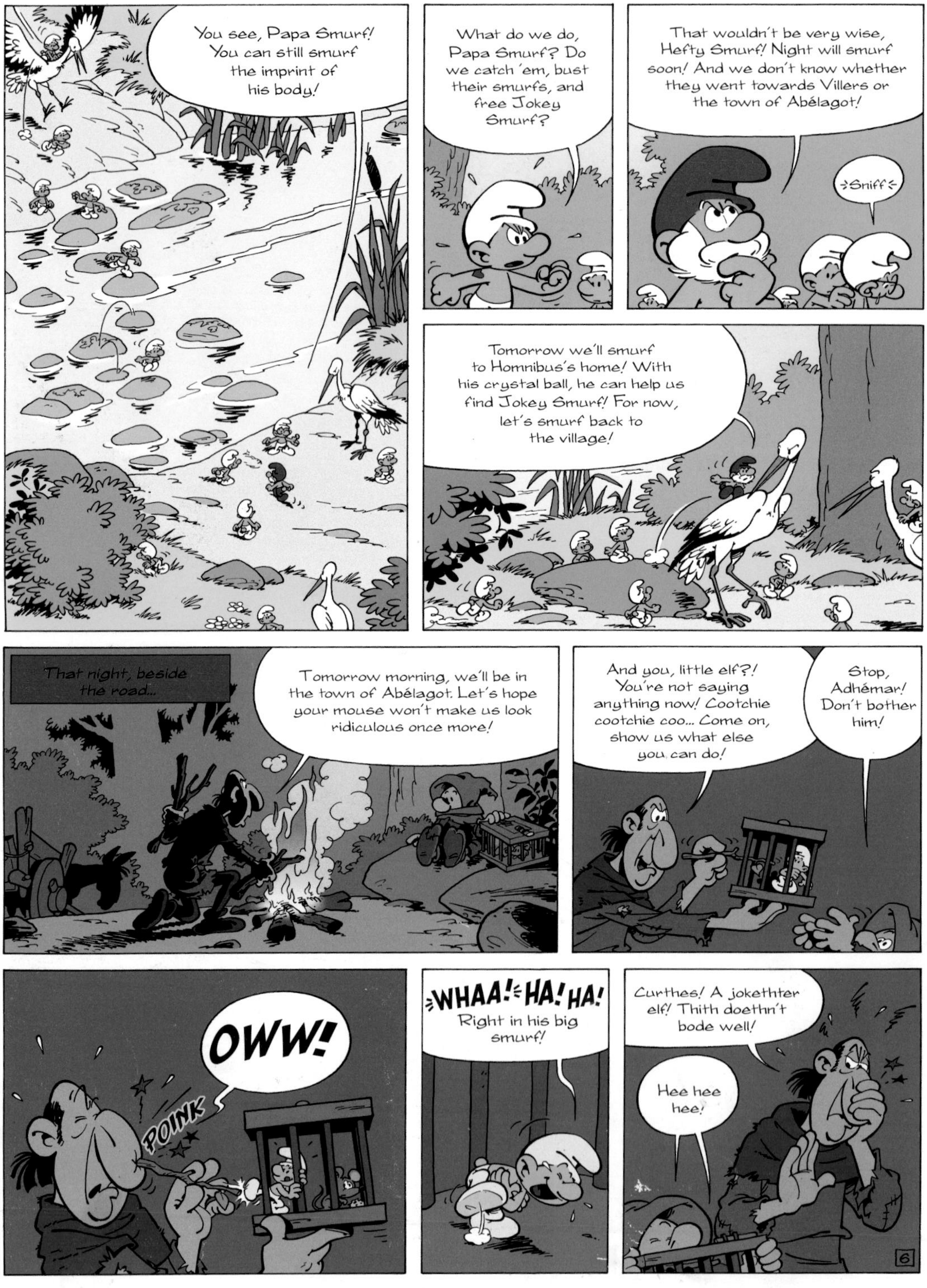
You see, Papa Smurf! You can still smurf the imprint of his body!
What do we do, Papa Smurf? Do we catch 'em, bust their smurfs, and free Jokey Smurf?
That wouldn't be very wise, Hefty Smurf! Night will smurf soon! And we don't know whether they went towards Villers or the town of Abélagot!
Sniff
Tomorrow we'll smurf to Homnibus's home! With his crystal ball, he can help us find Jokey Smurf! For now, let's smurf back to the village!
That night, beside the road...
Tomorrow morning, we'll be in the town of Abélagot. Let's hope your mouse won't make us look ridiculous once more!
And you, little elf?! You're not saying anything now! Cootchie cootchie coo... Come on, show us what else you can do!
Stop, Adhémar! Don't bother him!
OWW!
POINK
WHAA! HA! HA!
Right in his big smurf!
Curthes! A jokeththter elf! Thith doethn't bode well!
Hee hee hee!
6

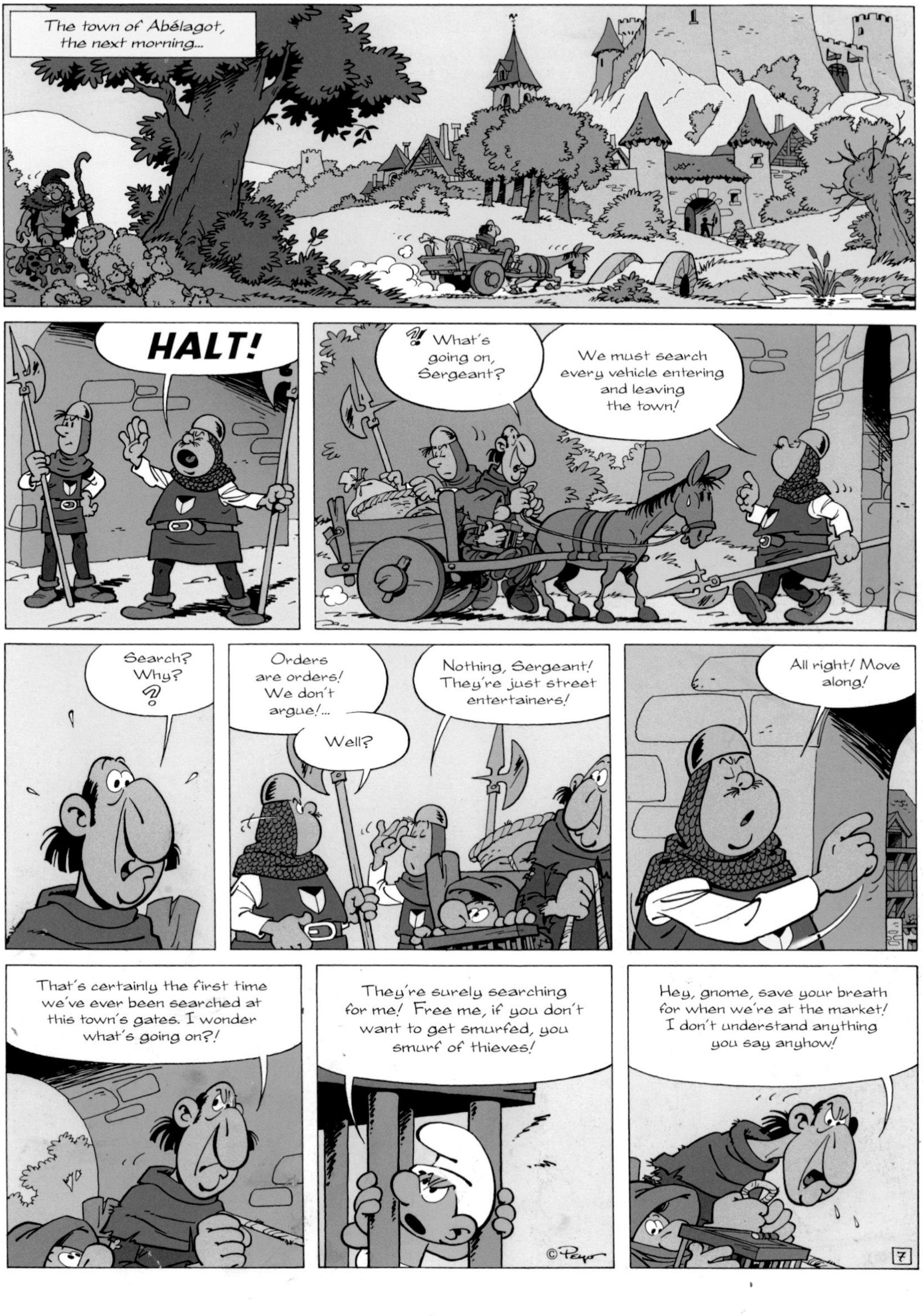
The town of Abélagot, the next morning...
HALT!
What's going on, Sergeant?
We must search every vehicle entering and leaving the town!
Search? Why?
Orders are orders! We don't argue!...
Well?
Nothing, Sergeant! They're just street entertainers!
All right! Move along!
That's certainly the first time we've ever been searched at this town's gates. I wonder what's going on?!
They're surely searching for me! Free me, if you don't want to get smurfed, you smurf of thieves!
© Peyo
Hey, gnome, save your breath for when we're at the market! I don't understand anything you say anyhow!
7

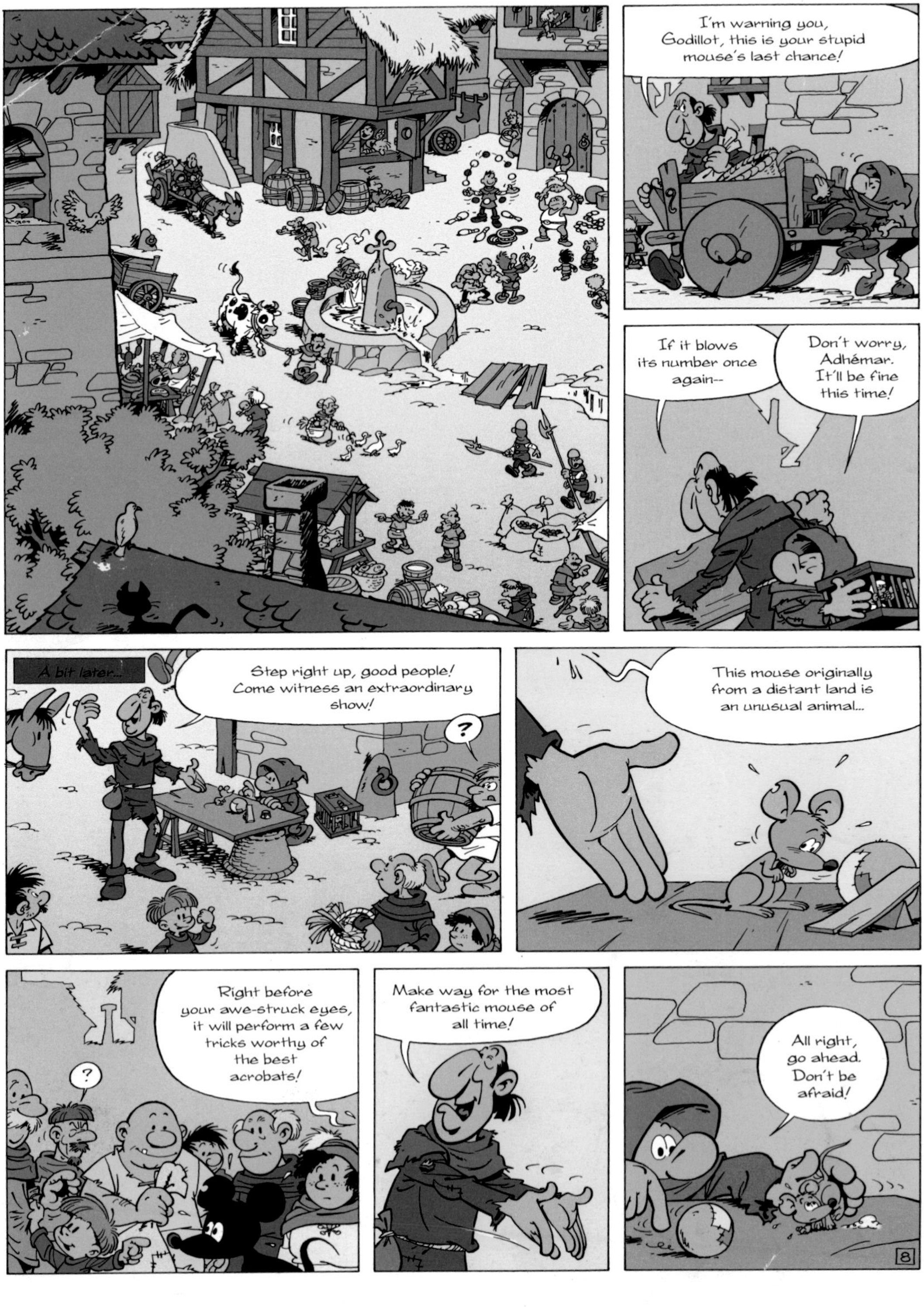
I'm warning you, Godillot, this is your stupid mouse's last chance!
If it blows its number once again--
Don't worry, Adhémar. It'll be fine this time!
A bit later...
Step right up, good people! Come witness an extraordinary show!
?
This mouse originally from a distant land is an unusual animal...
Right before your awe-struck eyes, it will perform a few tricks worthy of the best acrobats!
?
Make way for the most fantastic mouse of all time!
All right, go ahead. Don't be afraid!
8

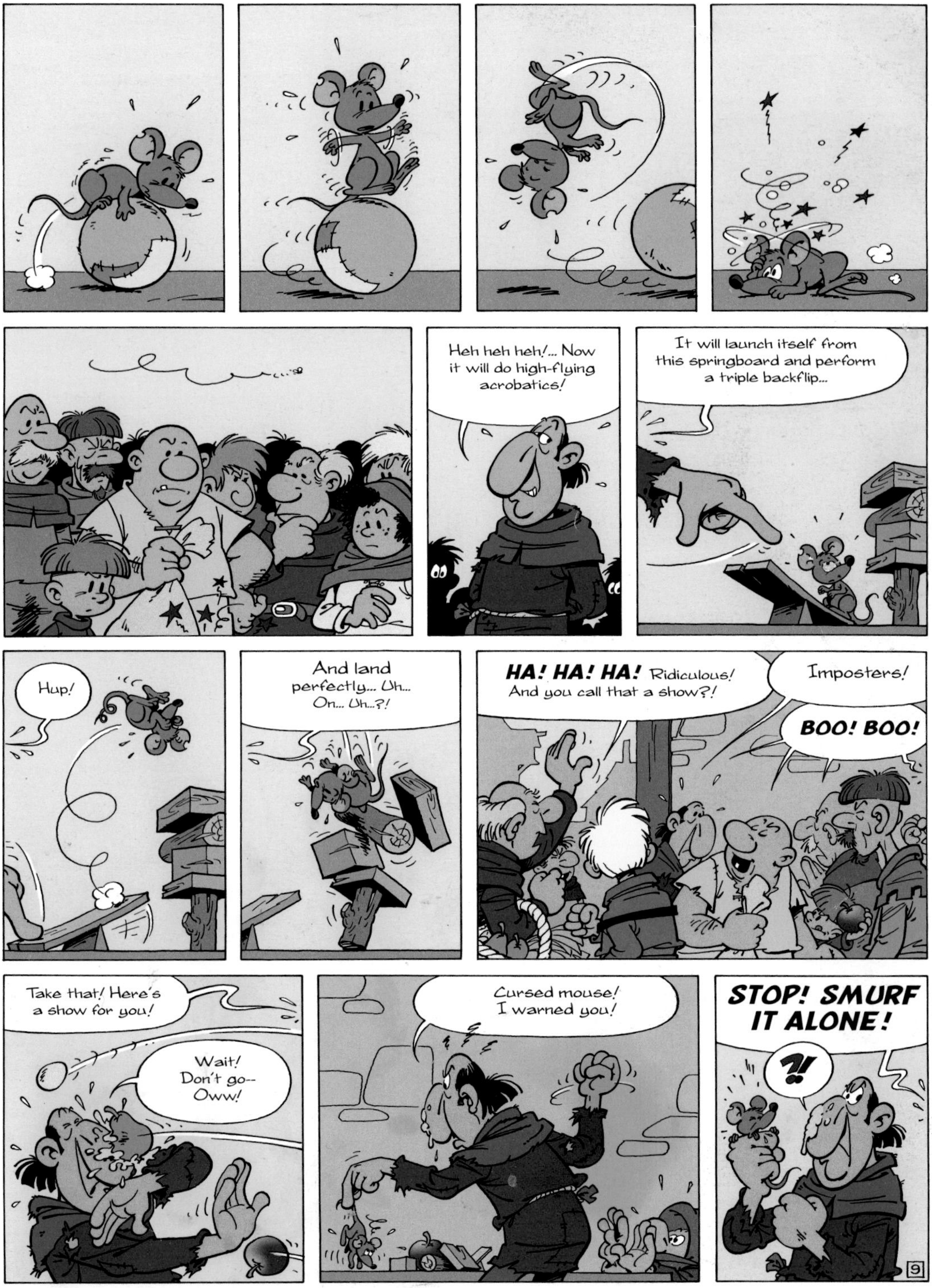
Heh heh heh!... Now it will do high-flying acrobatics!
It will launch itself from this springboard and perform a triple backflip...
Hup!
And land perfectly... Uh... On... Uh...?!
HA! HA! HA! Ridiculous! And you call that a show?!
Imposters!
BOO! BOO!
Take that! Here's a show for you!
Wait! Don't go-- Oww!
Cursed mouse! I warned you!
STOP! SMURF IT ALONE!
?!
9

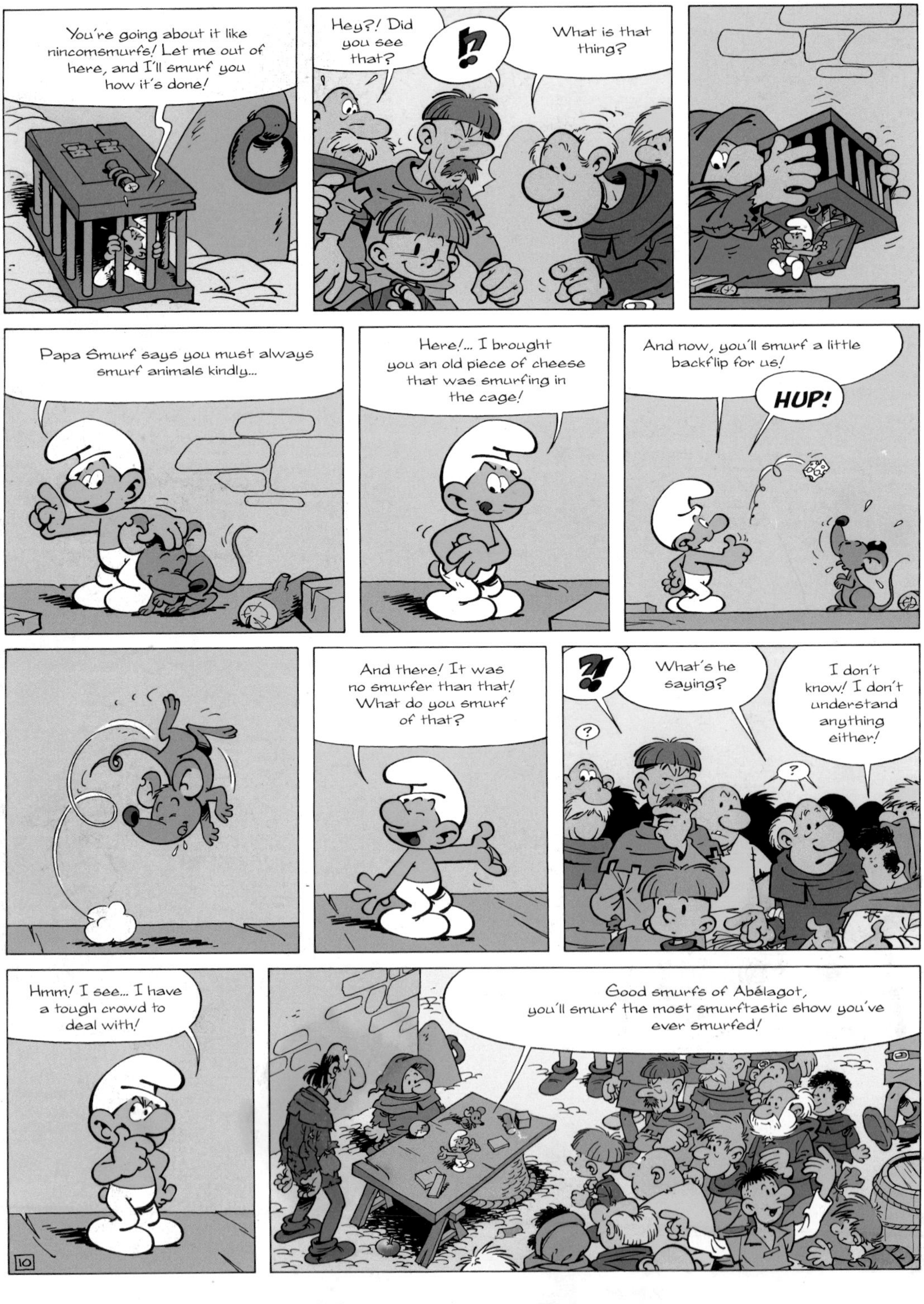
You're going about it like nincomsmurfs! Let me out of here, and I'll smurf you how it's done!
Hey?! Did you see that?
What is that thing?
Papa Smurf says you must always smurf animals kindly...
Here!... I brought you an old piece of cheese that was smurfing in the cage!
And now, you'll smurf a little backflip for us!
HUP!
And there! It was no smurfer than that! What do you smurf of that?
What's he saying?
I don't know! I don't understand anything either!
Hmm! I see... I have a tough crowd to deal with!
Good smurfs of Abélagot, you'll smurf the most smurftastic show you've ever smurfed!

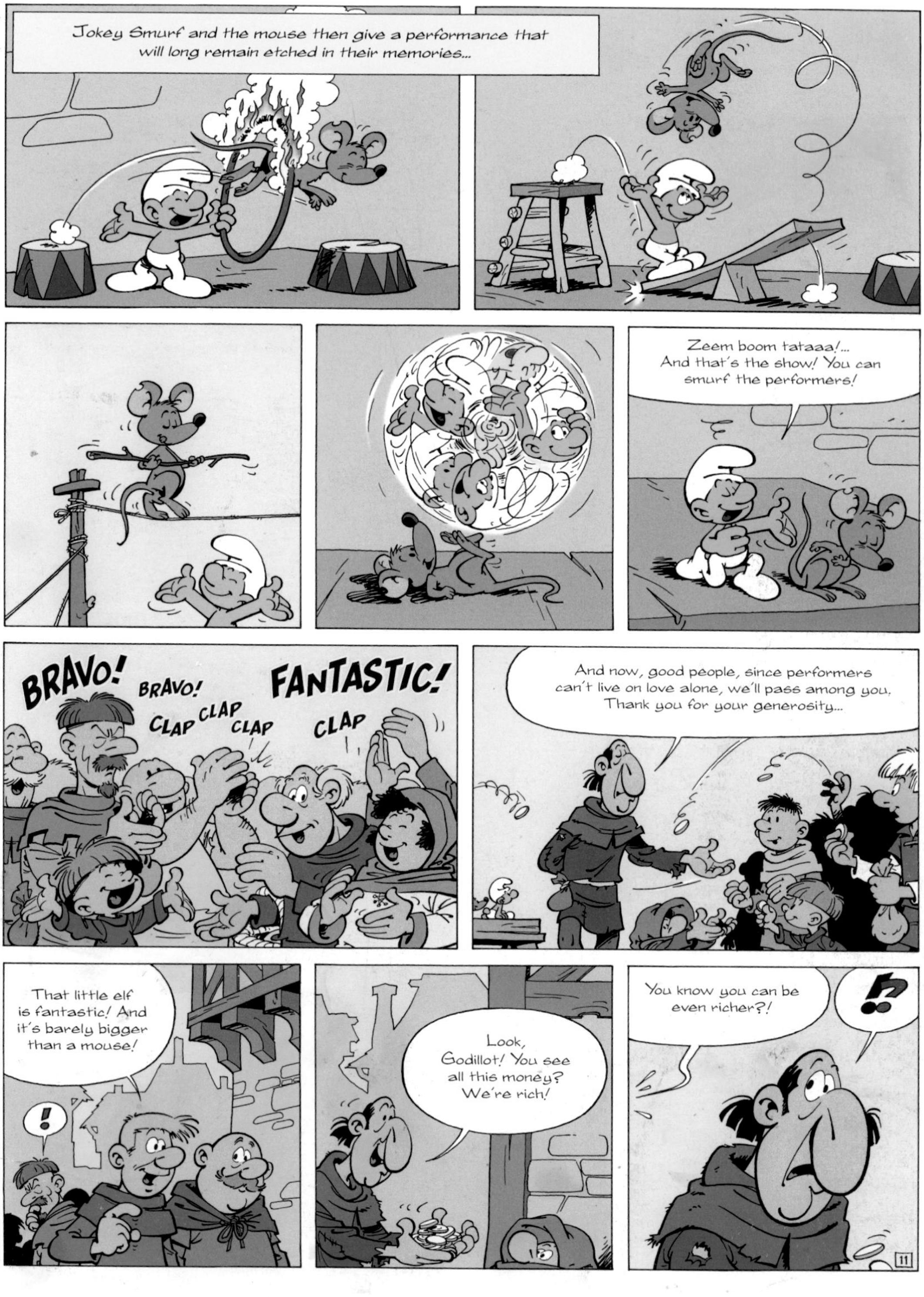
Jokey Smurf and the mouse then give a performance that will long remain etched in their memories...
Zeem boom tataaa!... And that's the show! You can smurf the performers!
BRAVO!
BRAVO!
CLAP CLAP CLAP
FANTASTIC!
CLAP
And now, good people, since performers can't live on love alone, we'll pass among you. Thank you for your generosity...
That little elf is fantastic! And it's barely bigger than a mouse!
!
Look, Godillot! You see all this money? We're rich!
You know you can be even richer?!
?!
11

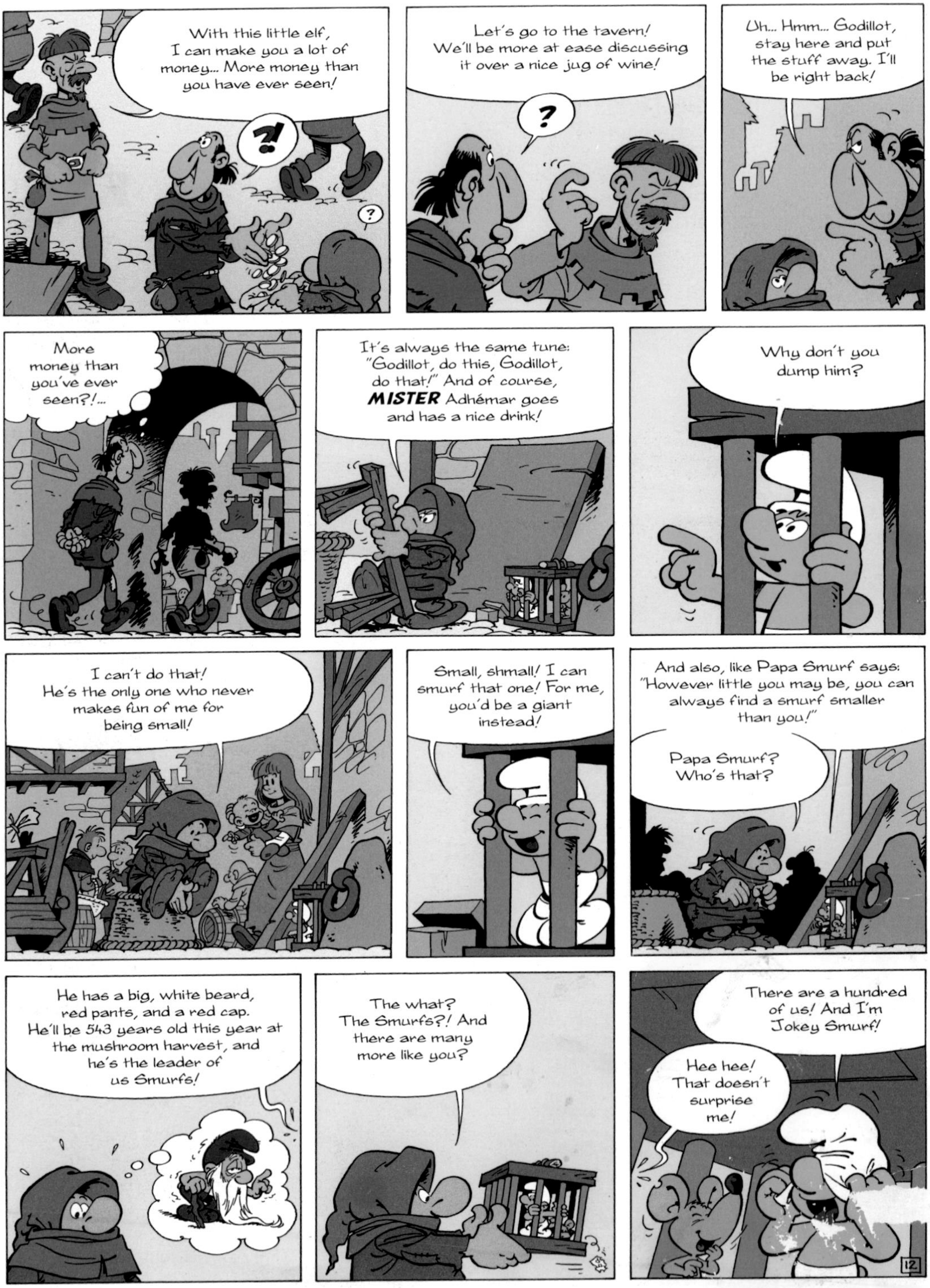
With this little elf, I can make you a lot of money... More money than you have ever seen!
?!
?
Let's go to the tavern! We'll be more at ease discussing it over a nice jug of wine!
?
Uh... Hmm... Godillot, stay here and put the stuff away. I'll be right back!
More money than you've ever seen?!...
It's always the same tune: "Godillot, do this, Godillot, do that!" And of course, MISTER Adhémar goes and has a nice drink!
Why don't you dump him?
I can't do that! He's the only one who never makes fun of me for being small!
Small, shmall! I can smurf that one! For me, you'd be a giant instead!
And also, like Papa Smurf says: "However little you may be, you can always find a smurf smaller than you!"
Papa Smurf? Who's that?
He has a big, white beard, red pants, and a red cap. He'll be 543 years old this year at the mushroom harvest, and he's the leader of us Smurfs!
The what? The Smurfs?! And there are many more like you?
There are a hundred of us! And I'm Jokey Smurf!
Hee hee! That doesn't surprise me!
12

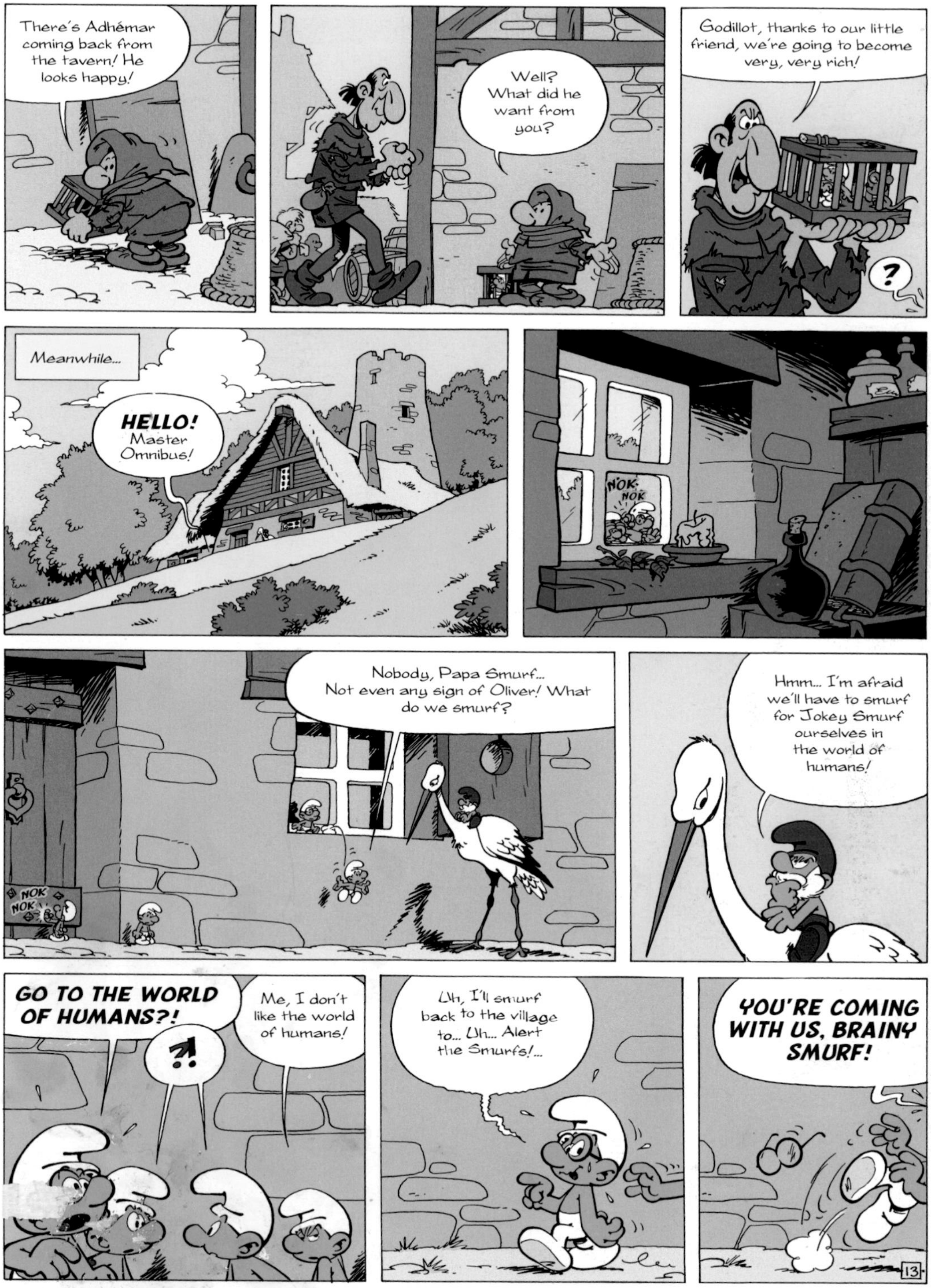
There's Adhémar coming back from the tavern! He looks happy!
Well? What did he want from you?
Godillot, thanks to our little friend, we're going to become very, very rich!
?
Meanwhile...
HELLO! Master Omnibus!
NOK NOK
Nobody, Papa Smurf... Not even any sign of Oliver! What do we smurf?
NOK NOK
Hmm... I'm afraid we'll have to smurf for Jokey Smurf ourselves in the world of humans!
GO TO THE WORLD OF HUMANS?!
?!
Me, I don't like the world of humans!
Uh, I'll smurf back to the village to... Uh... Alert the Smurfs!...
YOU'RE COMING WITH US, BRAINY SMURF!
13

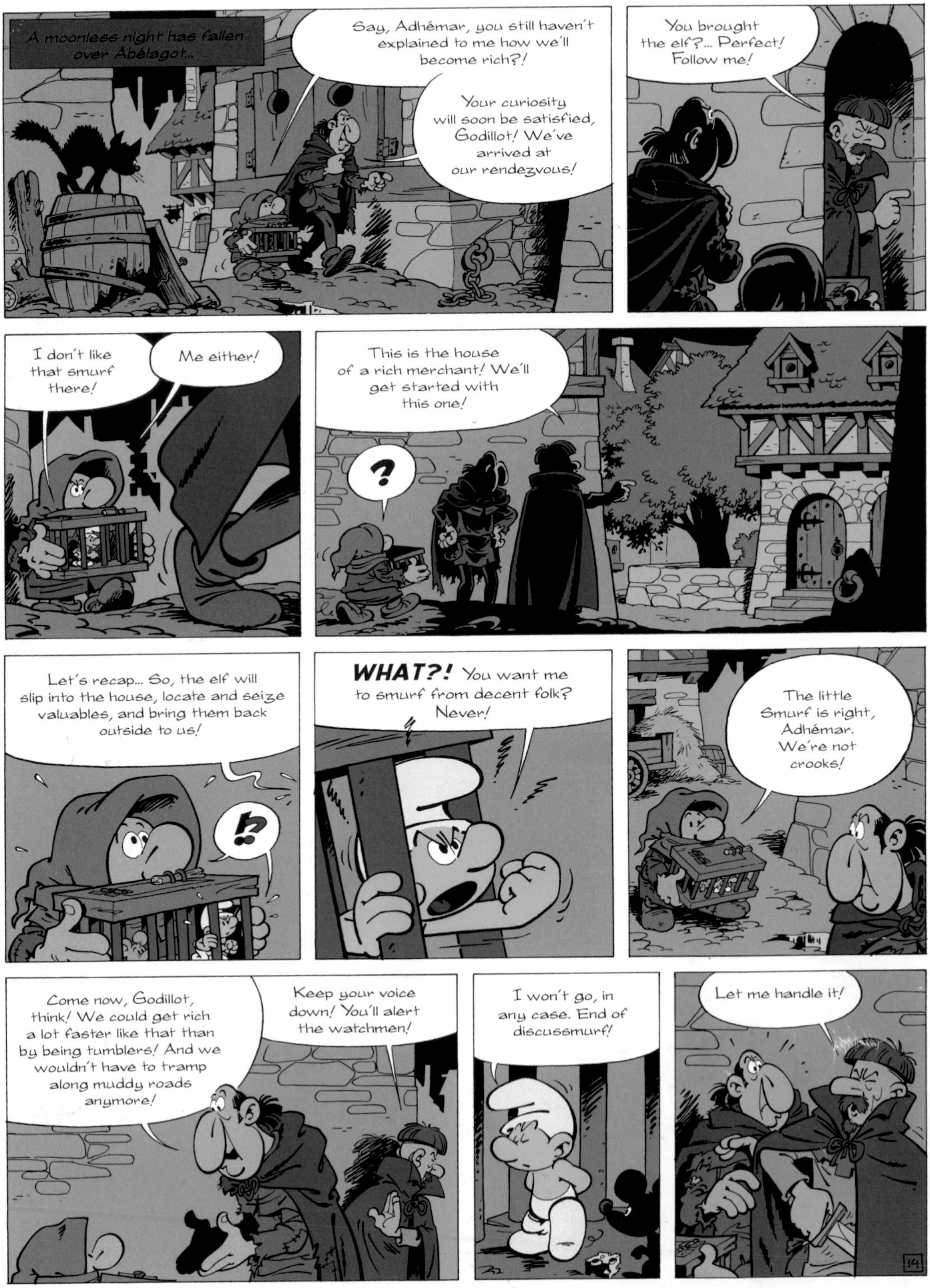

A moonless night has fallen over Abélagot...
Say, Adhémar, you still haven't explained to me how we'll become rich?!
Your curiosity will soon be satisfied, Godillot! We've arrived at our rendezvous!
You brought the elf?... Perfect! Follow me!
I don't like that smurf there!
Me either!
This is the house of a rich merchant! We'll get started with this one!
?
Let's recap... So, the elf will slip into the house, locate and seize valuables, and bring them back outside to us!
!?
WHAT?! You want me to smurf from decent folk? Never!
The little Smurf is right, Adhémar. We're not crooks!
Come now, Godillot, think! We could get rich a lot faster like that than by being tumblers! And we wouldn't have to tramp along muddy roads anymore!
Keep your voice down! You'll alert the watchmen!
I won't go, in any case. End of discussmurf!
Let me handle it!
14

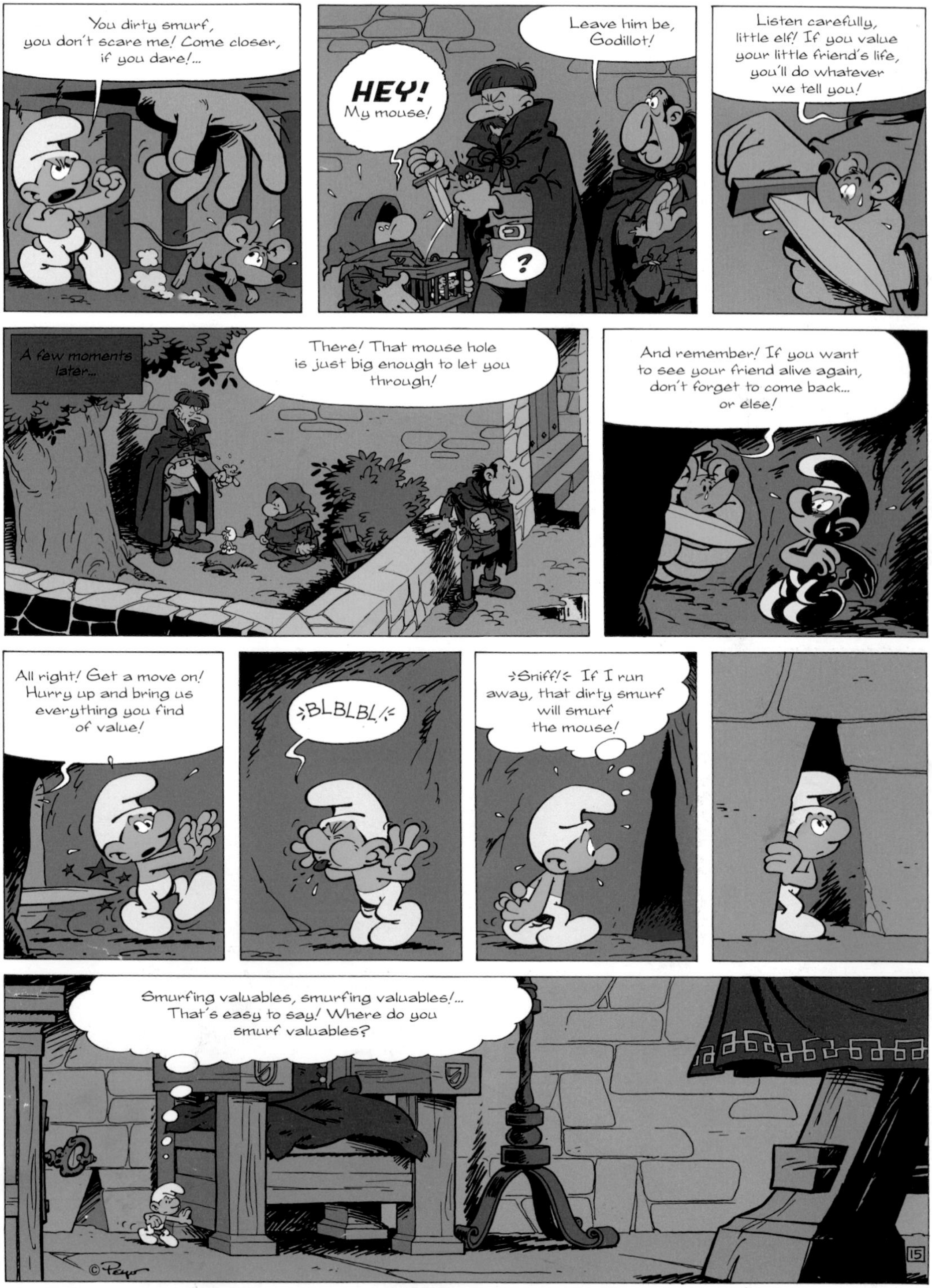
You dirty smurf, you don't scare me! Come closer, if you dare!...
HEY! My mouse!
Leave him be, Godillot!
?
Listen carefully, little elf! If you value your little friend's life, you'll do whatever we tell you!
A few moments later...
There! That mouse hole is just big enough to let you through!
And remember! If you want to see your friend alive again, don't forget to come back... or else!
All right! Get a move on! Hurry up and bring us everything you find of value!
BLBLBL!
Sniff! If I run away, that dirty smurf will smurf the mouse!
Smurfing valuables, smurfing valuables!... That's easy to say! Where do you smurf valuables?
15
©Peyo

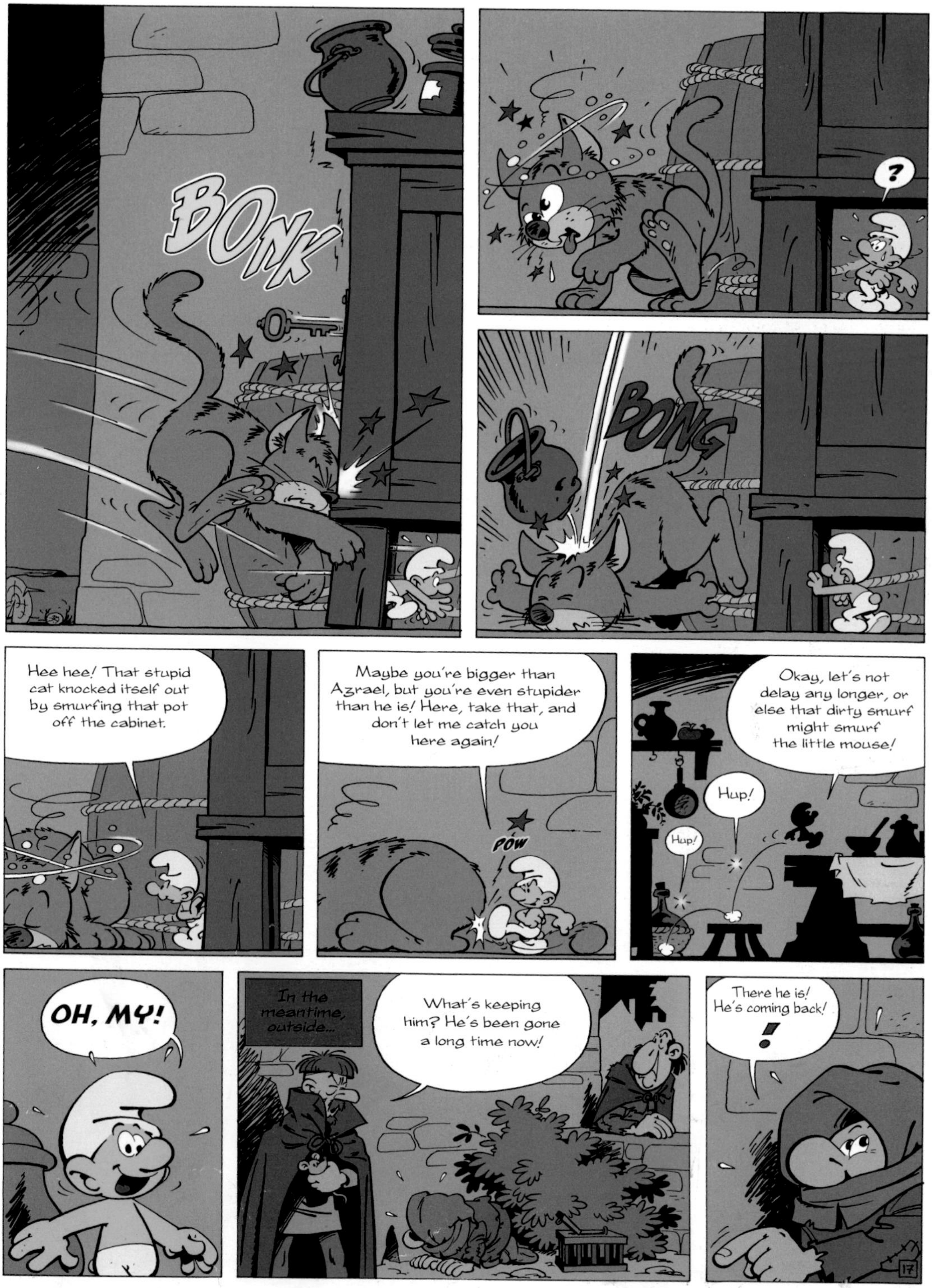
BONK
?
BONG
Hee hee! That stupid cat knocked itself out by smurfing that pot off the cabinet.
Maybe you're bigger than Azrael, but you're even stupider than he is! Here, take that, and don't let me catch you here again!
POW
Okay, let's not delay any longer, or else that dirty smurf might smurf the little mouse!
Hup!
Hup!
OH, MY!
In the meantime, outside...
What's keeping him? He's been gone a long time now!
There he is! He's coming back!
!
17

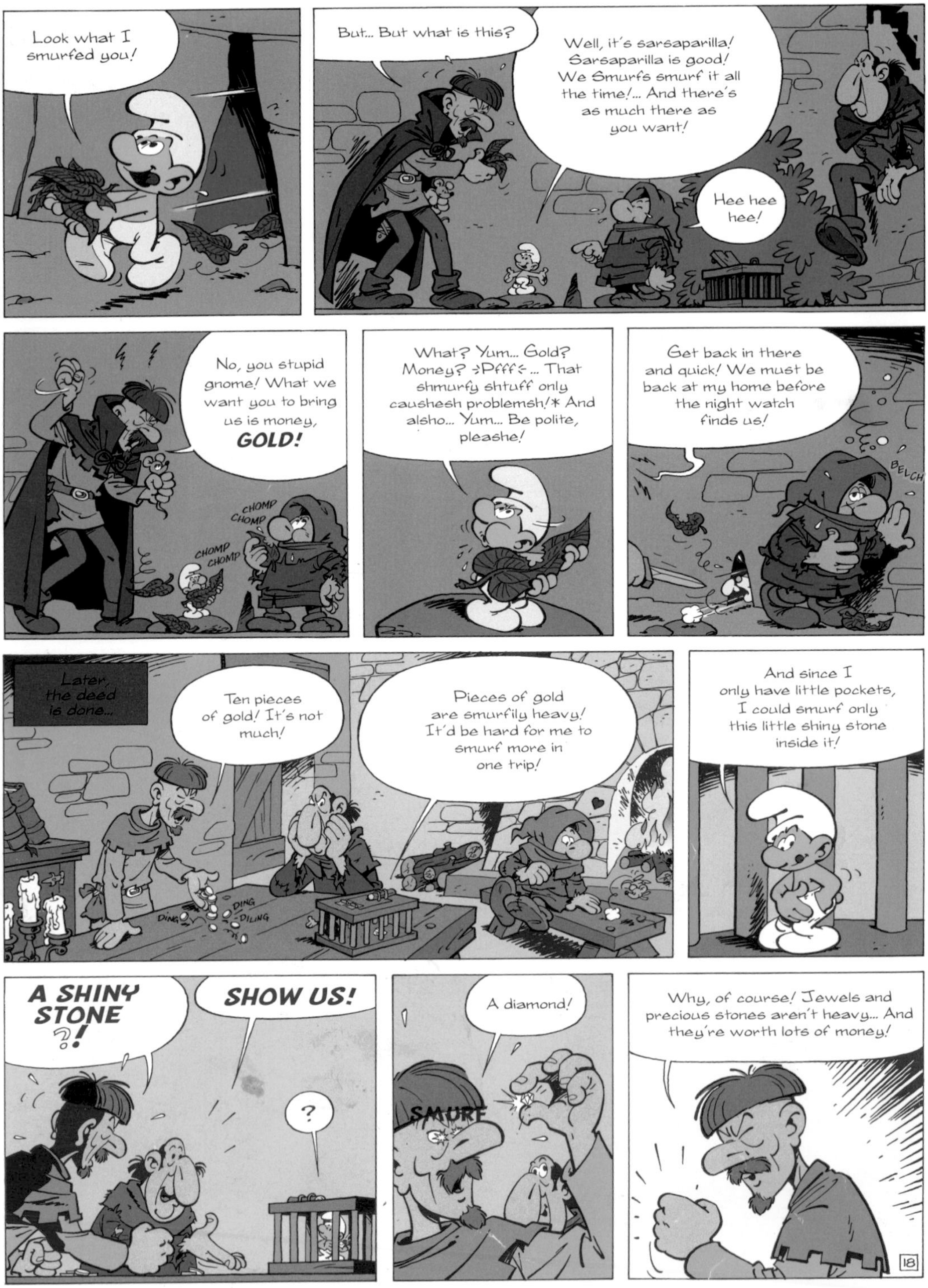
Look what I smurfed you!
But... But what is this?
Well, it's sarsaparilla! Sarsaparilla is good! We Smurfs smurf it all the time!... And there's as much there as you want!
Hee hee hee!
No, you stupid gnome! What we want you to bring us is money, GOLD!
CHOMP CHOMP
CHOMP CHOMP
What? Yum... Gold? Money? Pfff... That shmurfy shtuff only caushesh problemsh!* And alsho... Yum... Be polite, pleashe!
Get back in there and quick! We must be back at my home before the night watch finds us!
BELCH
Later, the deed is done...
Ten pieces of gold! It's not much!
DING DING DILING
Pieces of gold are smurfily heavy! It'd be hard for me to smurf more in one trip!
And since I only have little pockets, I could smurf only this little shiny stone inside it!
A SHINY STONE ?!
SHOW US!
?
A diamond!
SMURF
Why, of course! Jewels and precious stones aren't heavy... And they're worth lots of money!
18

*See THE SMURFS #18 "The Finance Smurf," if you don't believe us!

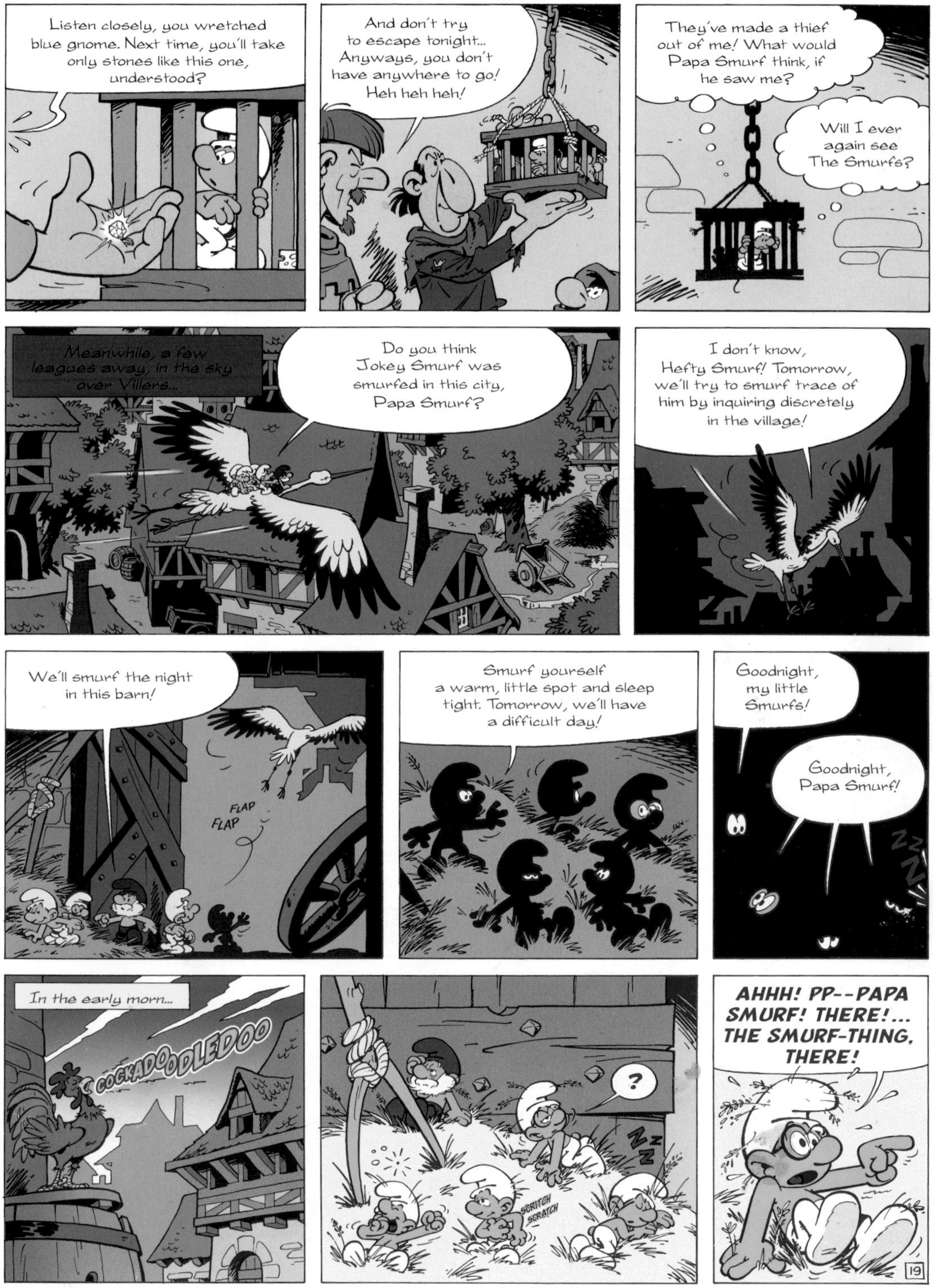

Listen closely, you wretched blue gnome. Next time, you'll take only stones like this one, understood?
And don't try to escape tonight... Anyways, you don't have anywhere to go! Heh heh heh!
They've made a thief out of me! What would Papa Smurf think, if he saw me?
Will I ever again see The Smurfs?
Meanwhile, a few leagues away, in the sky over Villers...
Do you think Jokey Smurf was smurfed in this city, Papa Smurf?
I don't know, Hefty Smurf! Tomorrow, we'll try to smurf trace of him by inquiring discretely in the village!
We'll smurf the night in this barn!
FLAP
FLAP
Smurf yourself a warm, little spot and sleep tight. Tomorrow, we'll have a difficult day!
Goodnight, my little Smurfs!
Goodnight, Papa Smurf!
In the early morn...
COCKADOODLEDOO
?
SCRITCH
SCRATCH
AHHH! PP--PAPA SMURF! THERE!... THE SMURF-THING, THERE!
19

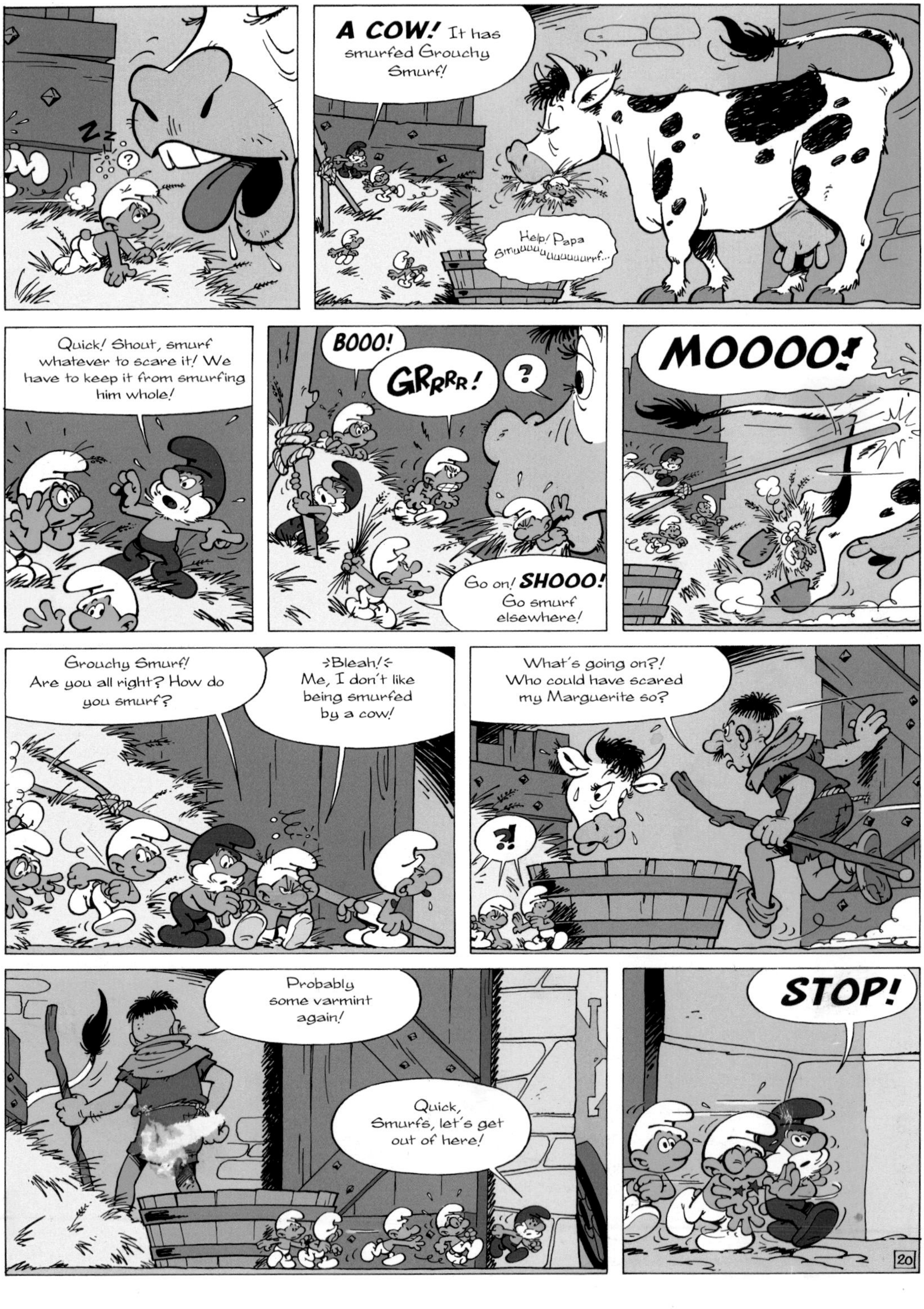

A COW! It has smurfed Grouchy Smurf!
Help! Papa Smuuuuuuuuuuurrf...
Quick! Shout, smurf whatever to scare it! We have to keep it from smurfing him whole!
BOOO!
GRRRR!
?
Go on! SHOOO! Go smurf elsewhere!
MOOOO!
Grouchy Smurf! Are you all right? How do you smurf?
Bleah! Me, I don't like being smurfed by a cow!
What's going on?! Who could have scared my Marguerite so?
?!
Probably some varmint again!
Quick, Smurfs, let's get out of here!
STOP!
20

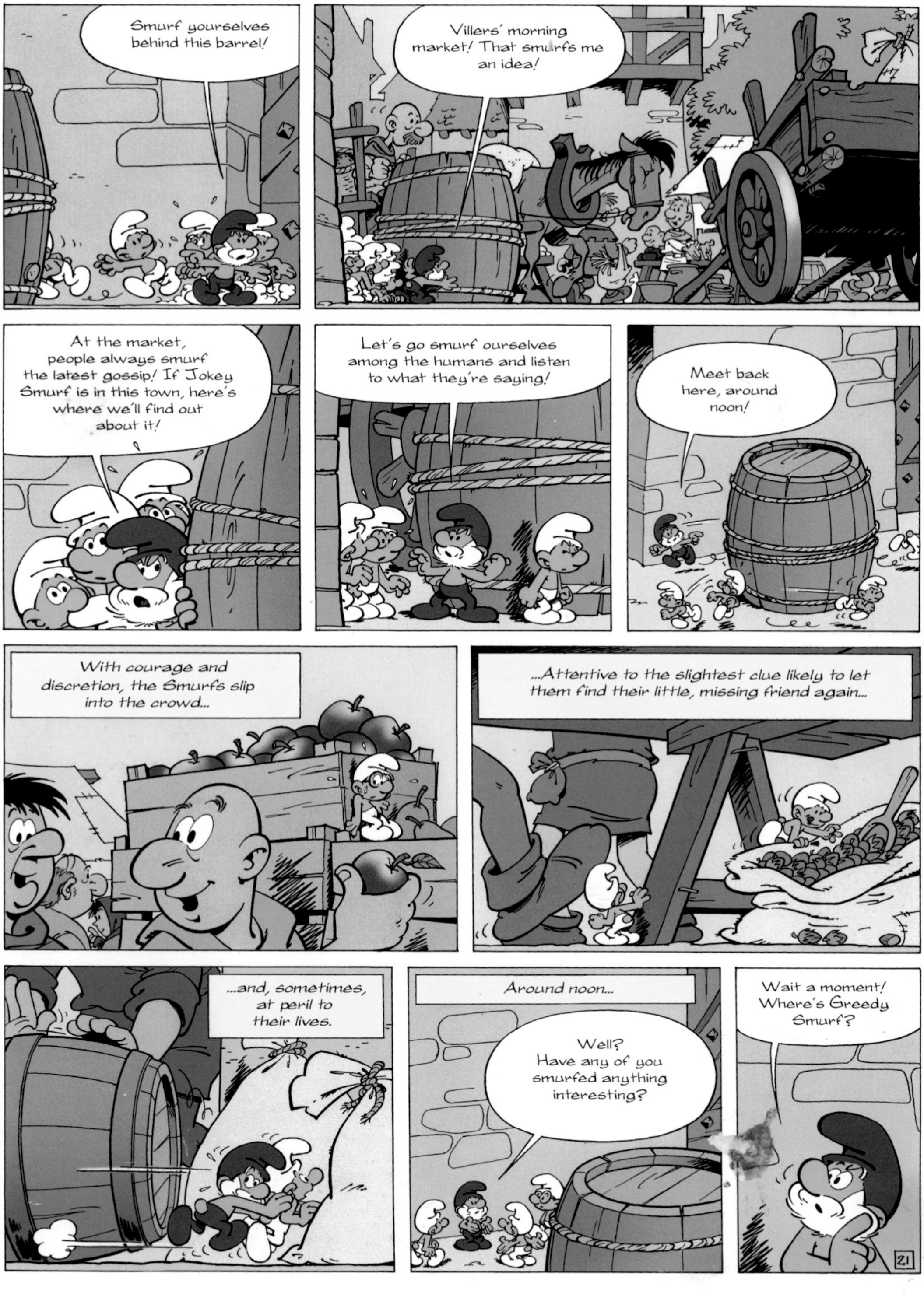

Smurf yourselves behind this barrel!
Villers' morning market! That smurfs me an idea!
At the market, people always smurf the latest gossip! If Jokey Smurf is in this town, here's where we'll find out about it!
Let's go smurf ourselves among the humans and listen to what they're saying!
Meet back here, around noon!
With courage and discretion, the Smurfs slip into the crowd...
...Attentive to the slightest clue likely to let them find their little, missing friend again...
...and, sometimes, at peril to their lives.
Around noon...
Well? Have any of you smurfed anything interesting?
Wait a moment! Where's Greedy Smurf?
21

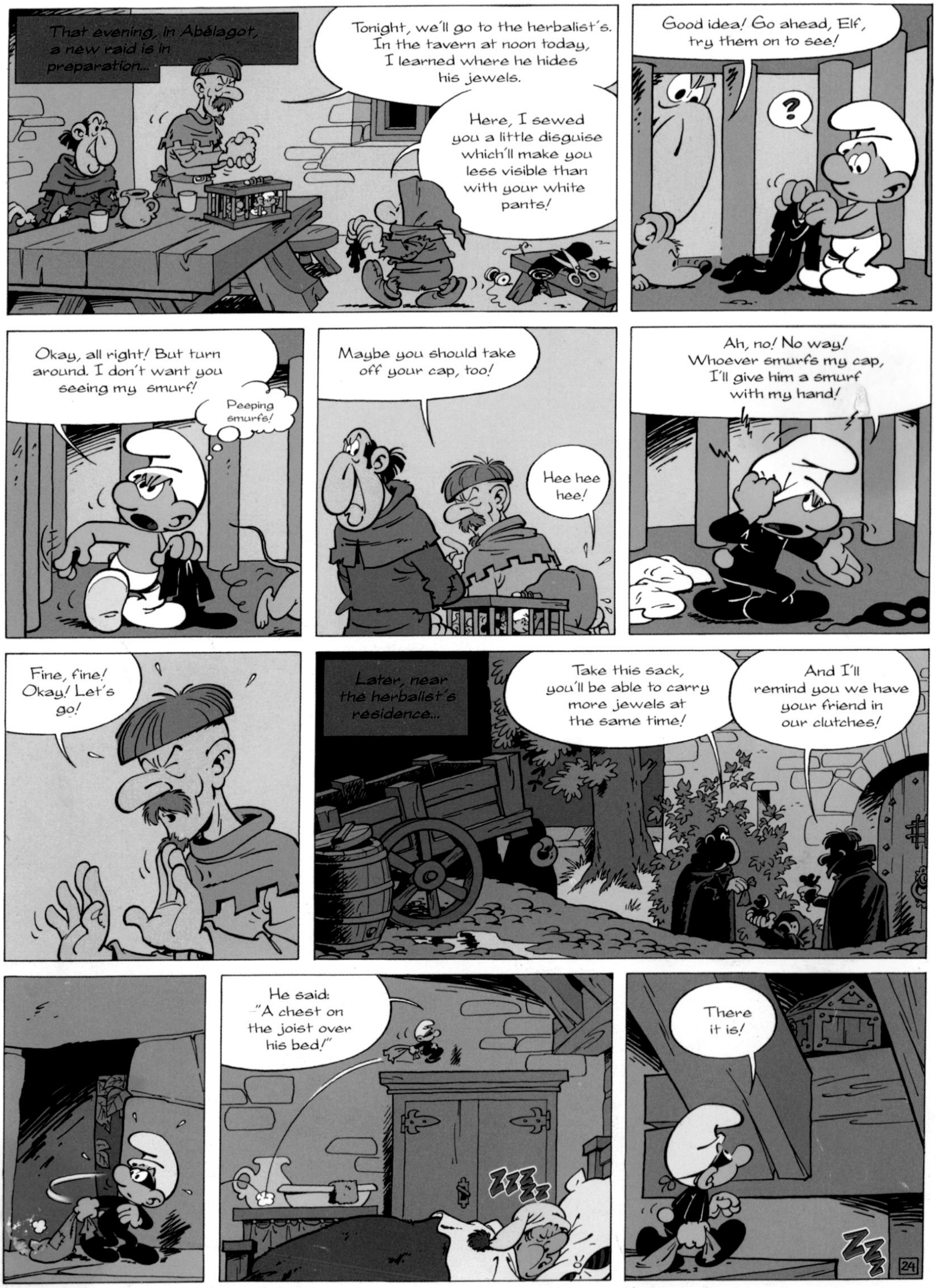
That evening, in Abélagot, a new raid is in preparation...
Tonight, we'll go to the herbalist's. In the tavern at noon today, I learned where he hides his jewels.
Here, I sewed you a little disguise which'll make you less visible than with your white pants!
Good idea! Go ahead, Elf, try them on to see!
?
Okay, all right! But turn around. I don't want you seeing my smurf!
Peeping smurfs!
Maybe you should take off your cap, too!
Hee hee hee!
Ah, no! No way! Whoever smurfs my cap, I'll give him a smurf with my hand!
Fine, fine! Okay! Let's go!
Later, near the herbalist's residence...
Take this sack, you'll be able to carry more jewels at the same time!
And I'll remind you we have your friend in our clutches!
He said: "A chest on the joist over his bed!"
ZZZZ
There it is!
ZZZ
24

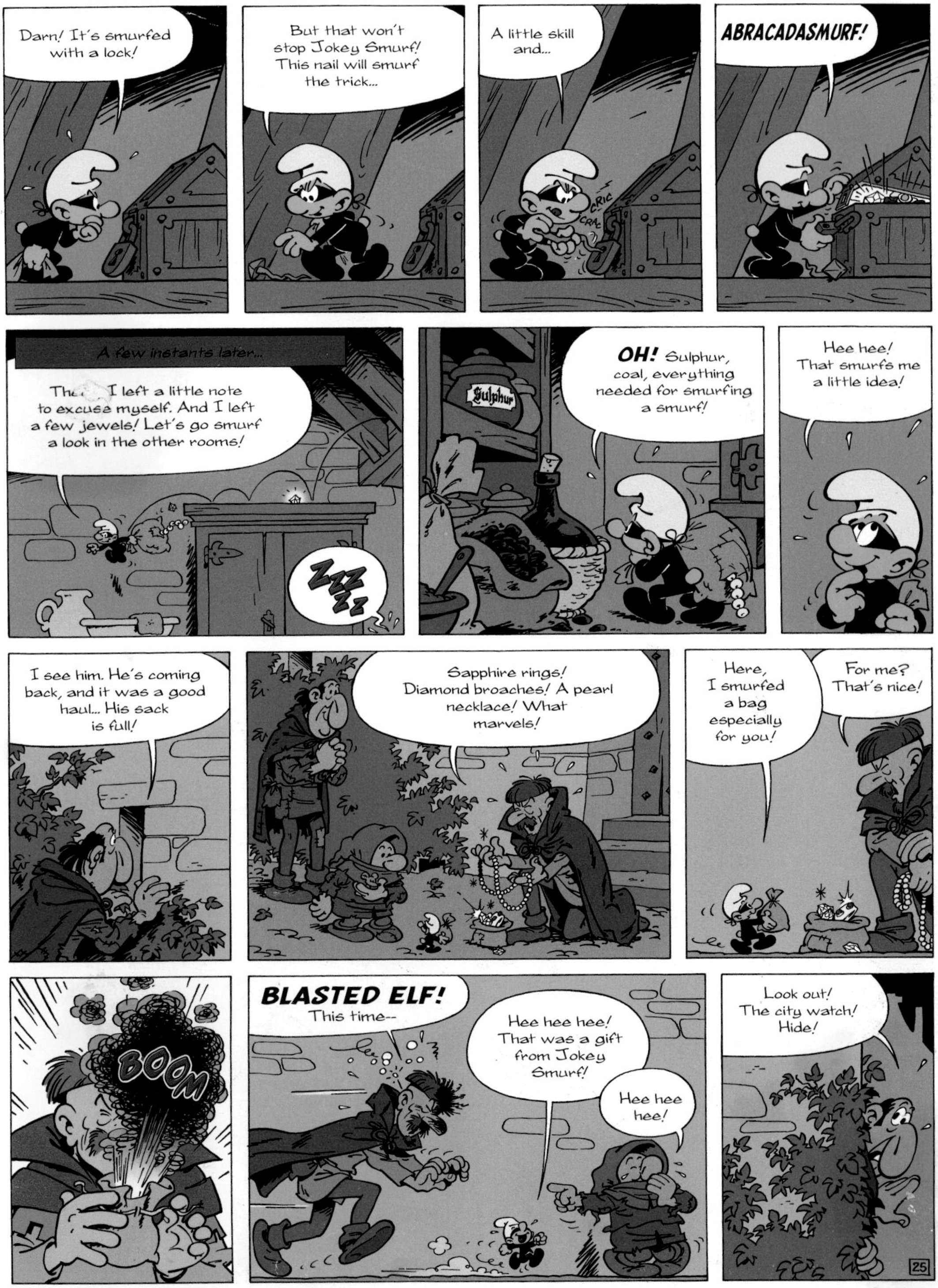
Darn! It's smurfed with a lock!
But that won't stop Jokey Smurf! This nail will smurf the trick...
A little skill and...
CRIC CRAC
ABRACADASMURF!
A few instants later...
I left a little note to excuse myself. And I left a few jewels! Let's go smurf a look in the other rooms!
ZZZ
Sulphur
OH! Sulphur, coal, everything needed for smurfing a smurf!
Hee hee! That smurfs me a little idea!
I see him. He's coming back, and it was a good haul... His sack is full!
Sapphire rings! Diamond broaches! A pearl necklace! What marvels!
Here, I smurfed a bag especially for you!
For me? That's nice!
BOOM
BLASTED ELF! This time--
Hee hee hee! That was a gift from Jokey Smurf!
Hee hee hee!
Look out! The city watch! Hide!
25

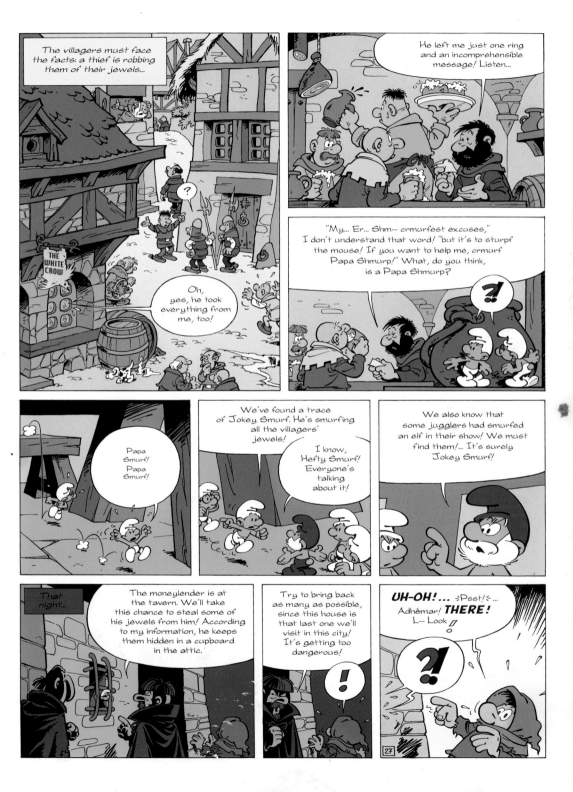

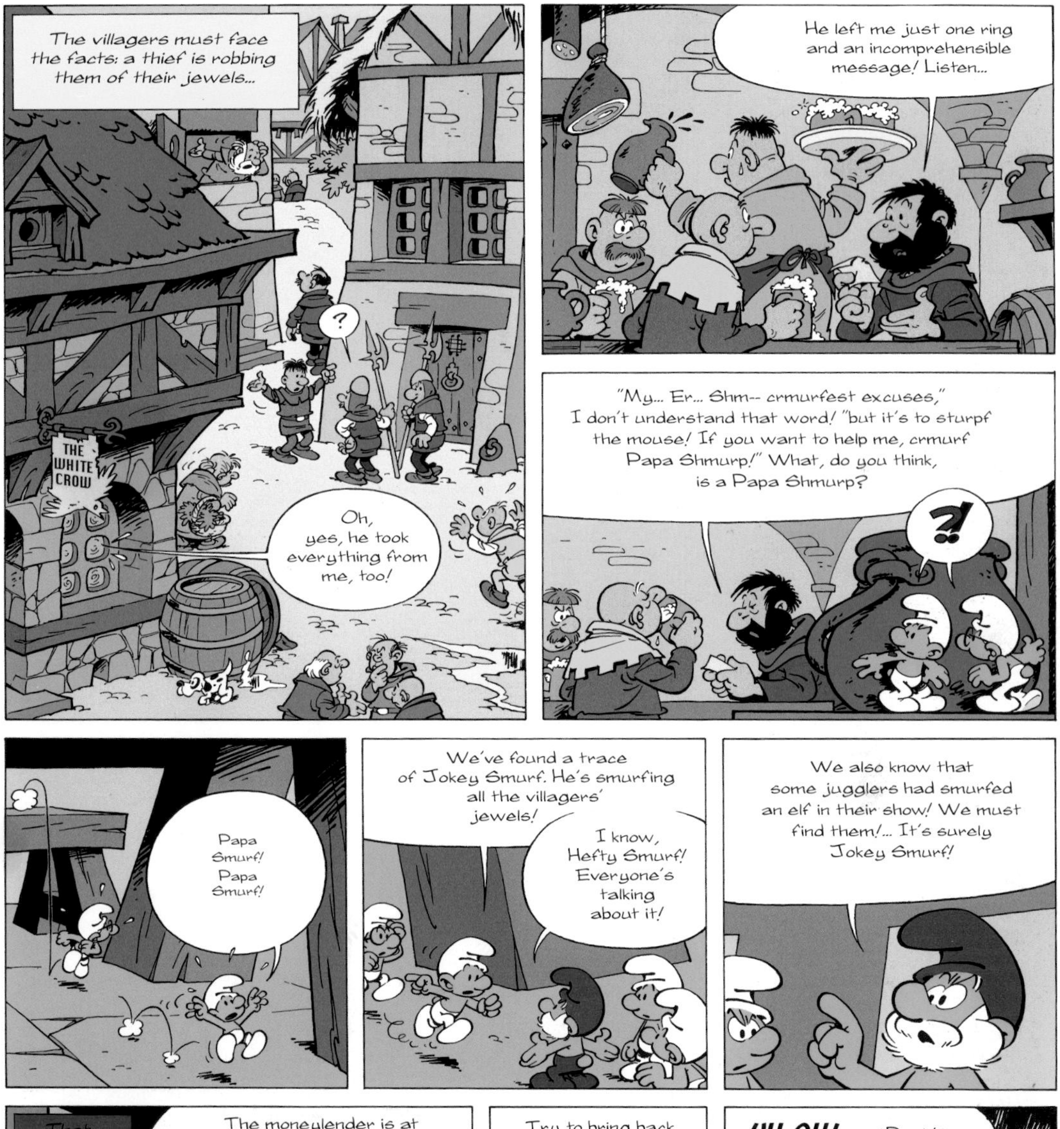
The villagers must face the facts: a thief is robbing them of their jewels...
THE WHITE CROW
?
Oh, yes, he took everything from me, too!
He left me just one ring and an incomprehensible message! Listen...
"My... Er... Shm-- crmurfest excuses," I don't understand that word! "but it's to sturpf the mouse! If you want to help me, crmurf Papa Shmurp!" What, do you think, is a Papa Shmurp?
?!
Papa Smurf! Papa Smurf!
We've found a trace of Jokey Smurf. He's smurfing all the villagers' jewels!
I know, Hefty Smurf! Everyone's talking about it!
We also know that some jugglers had smurfed an elf in their show! We must find them!... It's surely Jokey Smurf!
That night...
The moneylender is at the tavern. We'll take this chance to steal some of his jewels from him! According to my information, he keeps them hidden in a cupboard in the attic.
Try to bring back as many as possible, since this house is that last one we'll visit in this city! It's getting too dangerous!
!
UH-OH!... Psst!... Adhémar! THERE! L-- Look!
?!
27

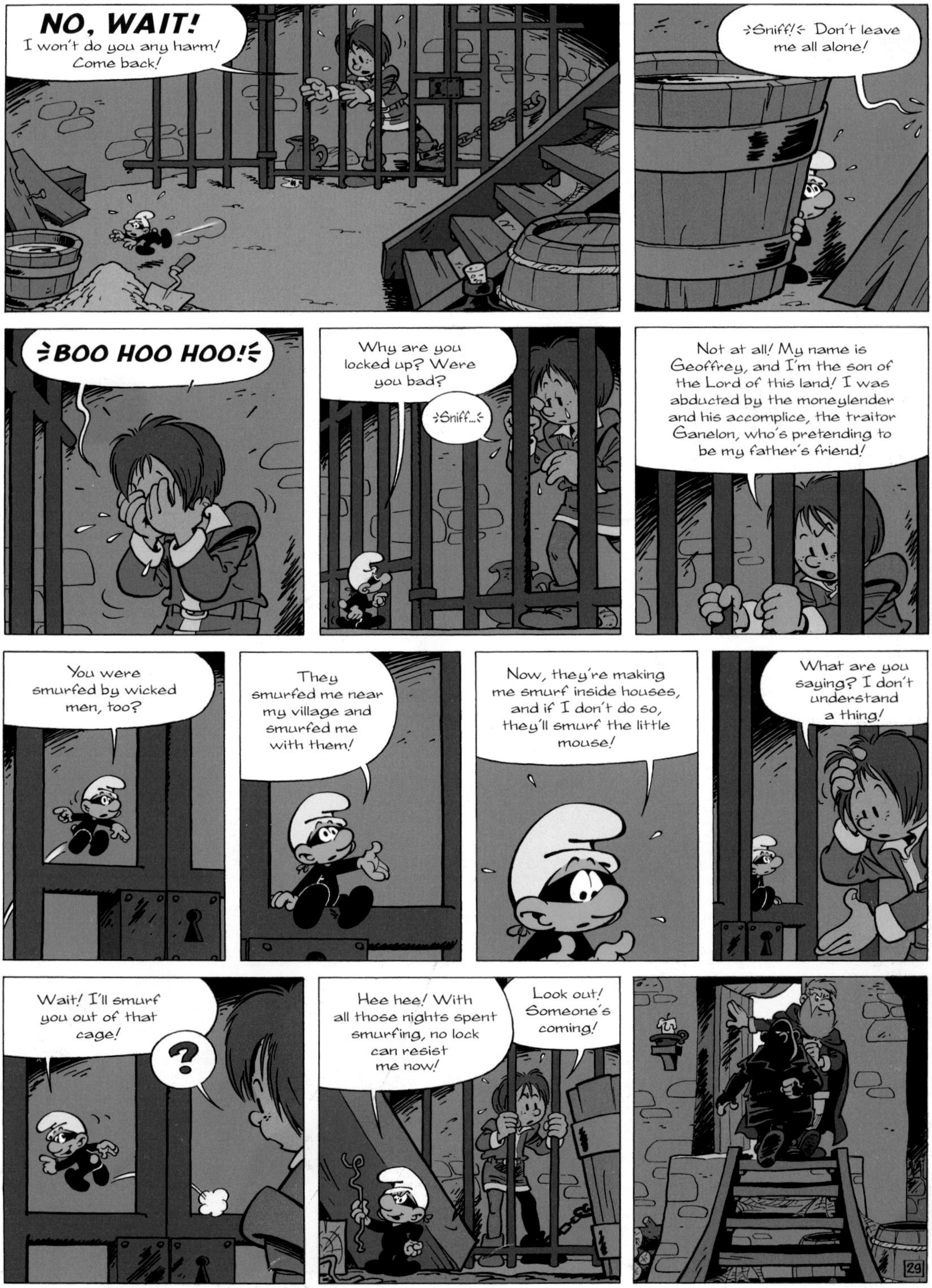

NO, WAIT! I won't do you any harm! Come back!
⁐Sniff!⁐ Don't leave me all alone!
⁐BOO HOO HOO!⁐
Why are you locked up? Were you bad?
⁐Sniff...⁐
Not at all! My name is Geoffrey, and I'm the son of the Lord of this land! I was abducted by the moneylender and his accomplice, the traitor Ganelon, who's pretending to be my father's friend!
You were smurfed by wicked men, too?
They smurfed me near my village and smurfed me with them!
Now, they're making me smurf inside houses, and if I don't do so, they'll smurf the little mouse!
What are you saying? I don't understand a thing!
Wait! I'll smurf you out of that cage!
?
Hee hee! With all those nights spent smurfing, no lock can resist me now!
Look out! Someone's coming!
29

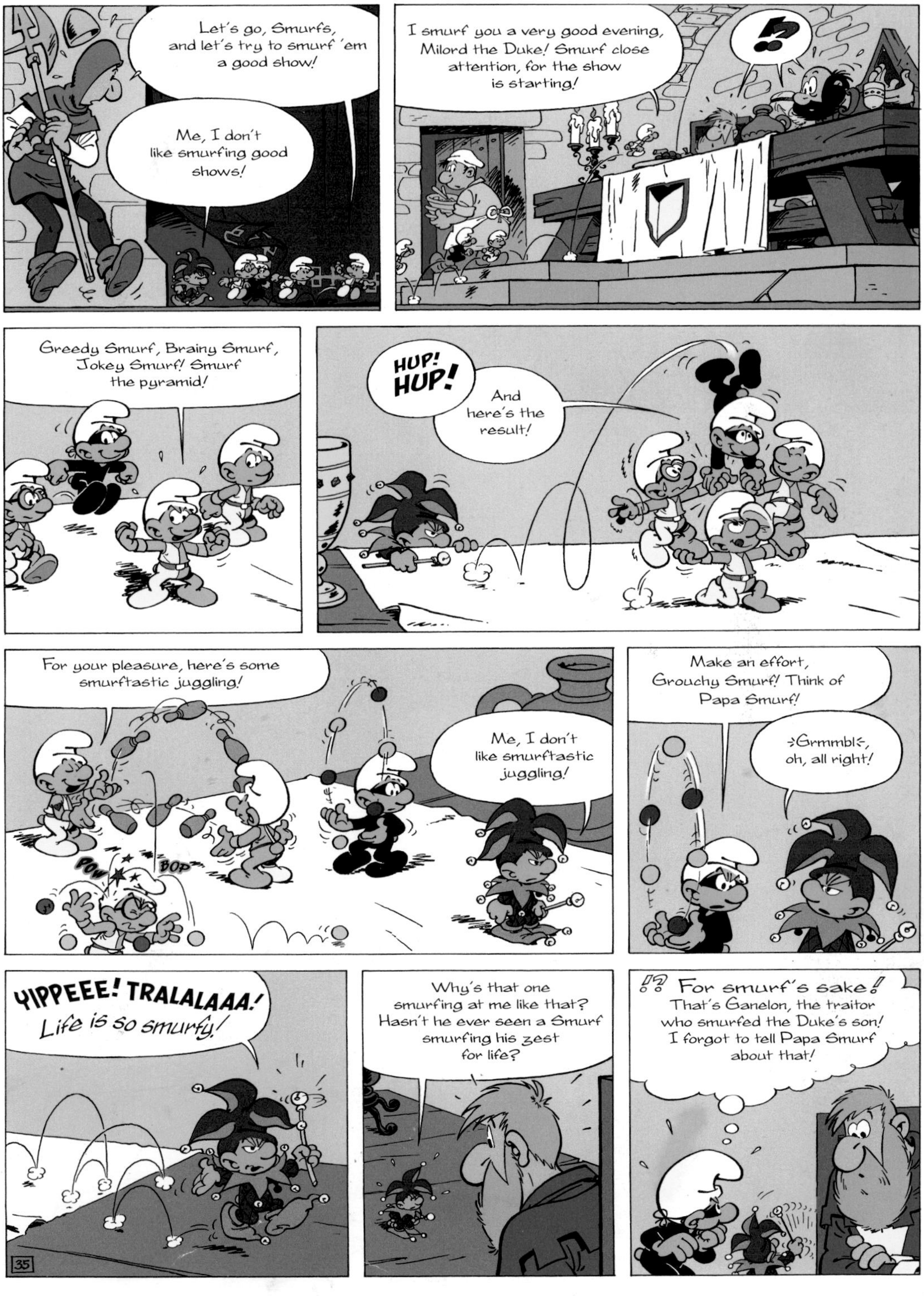
Let's go, Smurfs, and let's try to smurf 'em a good show!
Me, I don't like smurfing good shows!
I smurf you a very good evening, Milord the Duke! Smurf close attention, for the show is starting!
Greedy Smurf, Brainy Smurf, Jokey Smurf! Smurf the pyramid!
HUP! HUP!
And here's the result!
For your pleasure, here's some smurftastic juggling!
POW
BOP
Me, I don't like smurftastic juggling!
Make an effort, Grouchy Smurf! Think of Papa Smurf!
>Grmmbl<, oh, all right!
YIPPEEE! TRALALAAA! Life is so smurfy!
35
Why's that one smurfing at me like that? Hasn't he ever seen a Smurf smurfing his zest for life?
!? For smurf's sake! That's Ganelon, the traitor who smurfed the Duke's son! I forgot to tell Papa Smurf about that!

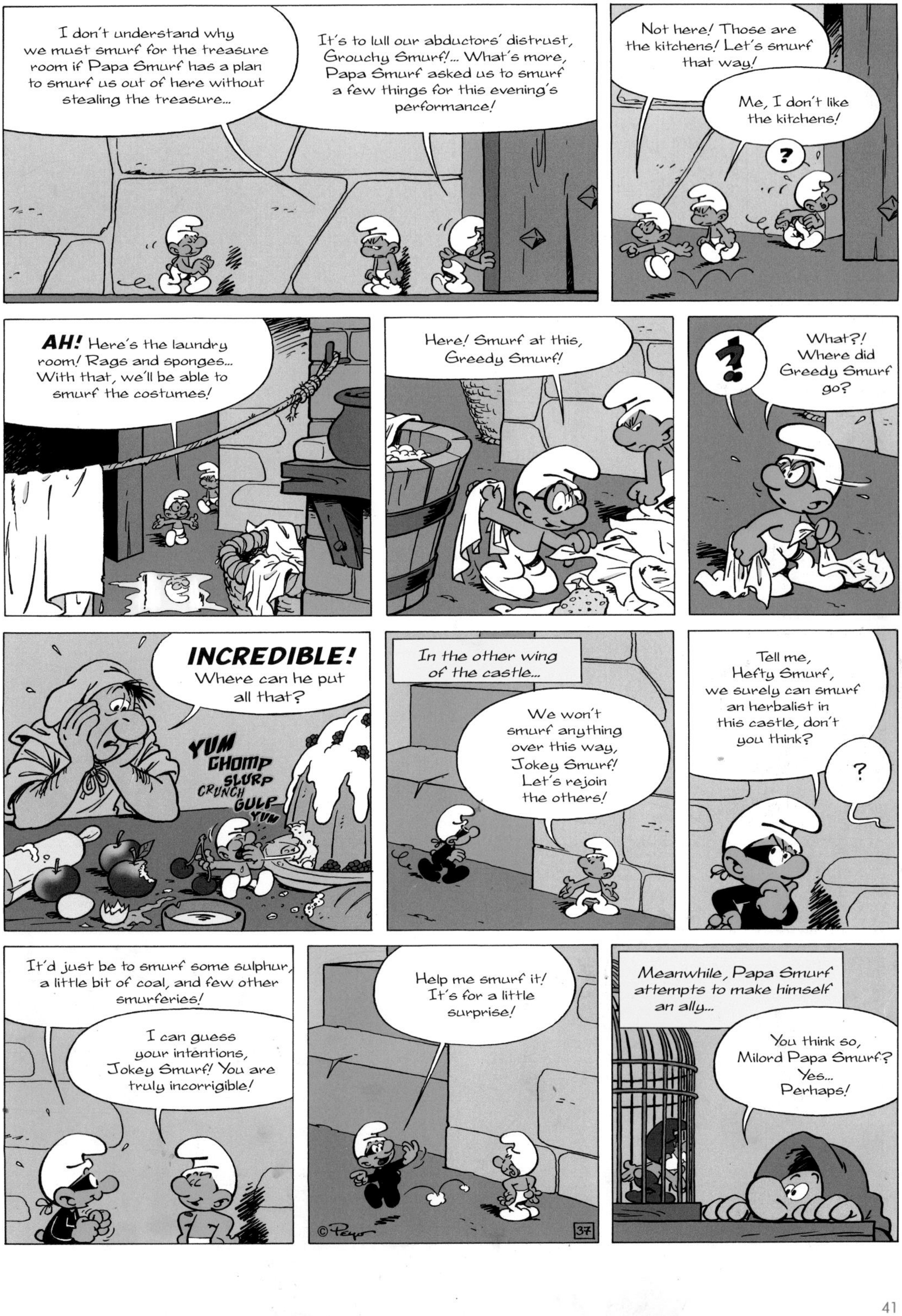
I don't understand why we must smurf for the treasure room if Papa Smurf has a plan to smurf us out of here without stealing the treasure...
It's to lull our abductors' distrust, Grouchy Smurf!... What's more, Papa Smurf asked us to smurf a few things for this evening's performance!
Not here! Those are the kitchens! Let's smurf that way!
Me, I don't like the kitchens!
?
AH! Here's the laundry room! Rags and sponges... With that, we'll be able to smurf the costumes!
Here! Smurf at this, Greedy Smurf!
?!
What?! Where did Greedy Smurf go?
INCREDIBLE! Where can he put all that?
YUM
CHOMP
SLURP
CRUNCH
GULP
YUM
In the other wing of the castle...
We won't smurf anything over this way, Jokey Smurf! Let's rejoin the others!
Tell me, Hefty Smurf, we surely can smurf an herbalist in this castle, don't you think?
?
It'd just be to smurf some sulphur, a little bit of coal, and few other smurferies!
I can guess your intentions, Jokey Smurf! You are truly incorrigible!
Help me smurf it! It's for a little surprise!
©Peyo
37
Meanwhile, Papa Smurf attempts to make himself an ally...
You think so, Milord Papa Smurf? Yes... Perhaps!

44

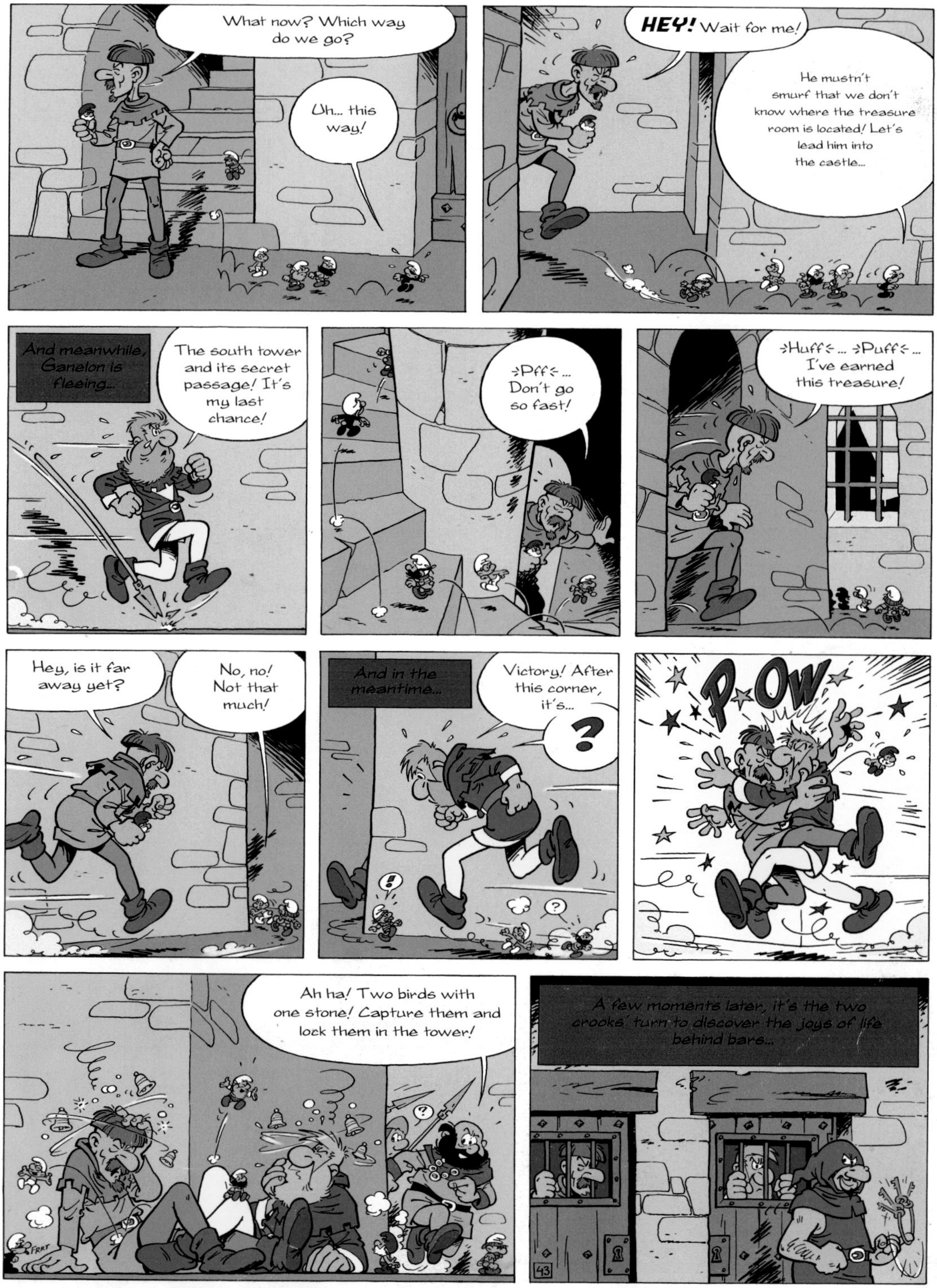
What now? Which way do we go?
Uh... this way!
HEY! Wait for me!
He mustn't smurf that we don't know where the treasure room is located! Let's lead him into the castle...
And meanwhile, Ganelon is fleeing...
The south tower and its secret passage! It's my last chance!
>Pff<... Don't go so fast!
>Huff<... >Puff<... I've earned this treasure!
Hey, is it far away yet?
No, no! Not that much!
And in the meantime...
Victory! After this corner, it's...
?
!
?
POW
FRRT
Ah ha! Two birds with one stone! Capture them and lock them in the tower!
?
A few moments later, it's the two crooks' turn to discover the joys of life behind bars...
43

48

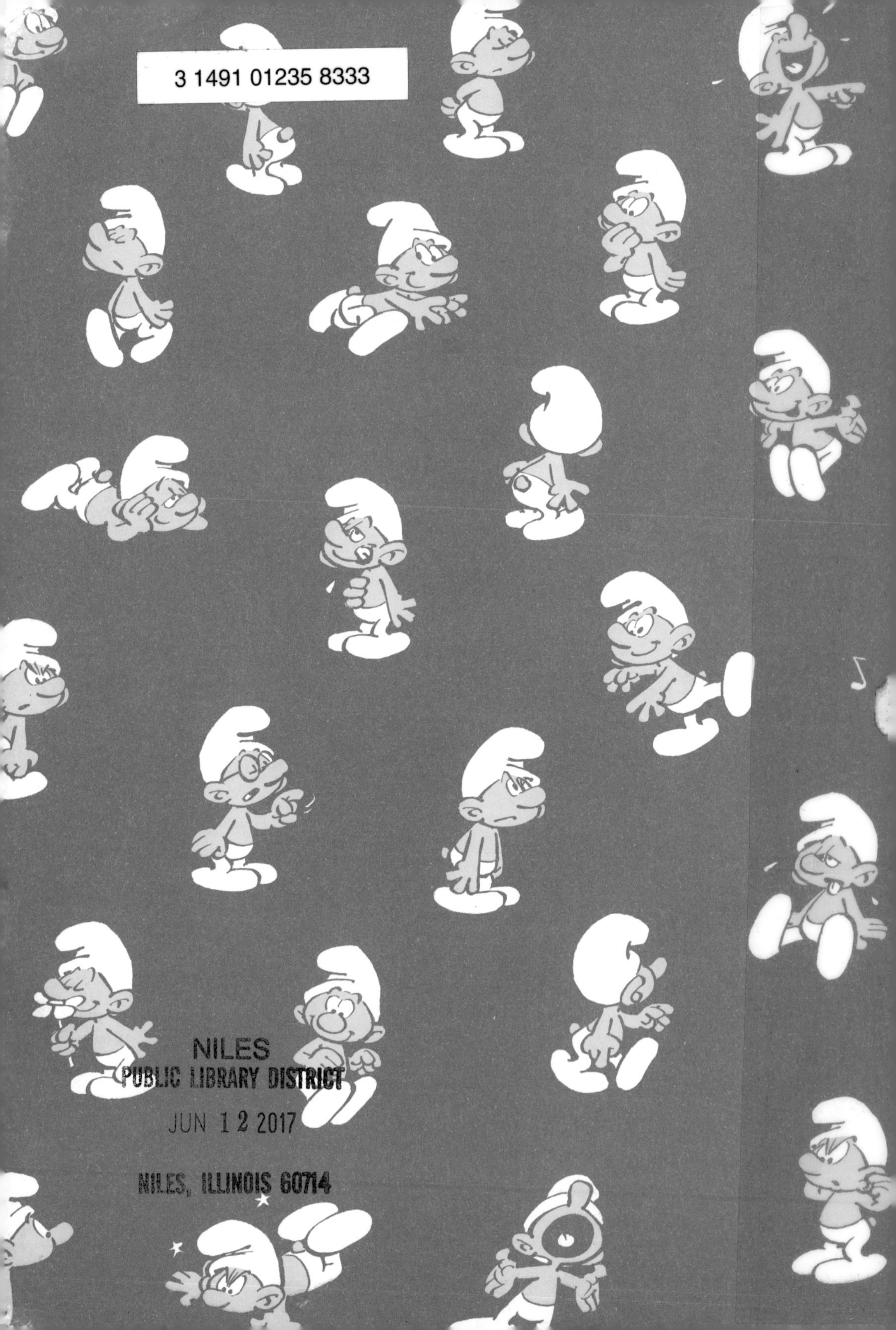